The MAYPOP KIDNAPPING

The
MAYPOP
KIDNAPPING

BY C. M. Surrisi

🌿 Carolrhoda Books • Minneapolis

Text copyright © 2016 by Cynthia Surrisi
Jacket illustration © 2016 by Gilbert Ford
Map design by Ingrid Sundberg

Carolrhoda Books
A division of Lerner Publishing Group, Inc.
241 First Avenue North
Minneapolis, MN 55401 USA

For reading levels and more information, look up this title at www.lernerbooks.com.

Backgrounds interior: © Gordan/Bigstock.com.

Main body text set in Bembo Std 12.5/17. Typeface provided by Monotype.

Library of Congress Cataloging-in-Publication Data

Surrisi, Cynthia.
        The Maypop kidnapping / C.M. Surrisi.
            pages cm
        Summary: "Quinnie's teacher has disappeared. Quinnie suspects a kidnapping but her mom, even though she's the sheriff of their small Maine town, disagrees. So Quinnie teams with her glamorous new neighbor to investigate the mystery" —Provided by publisher.
            ISBN 978-1-4677-5789-8 (lb : alk. paper) — ISBN 978-1-4677-9560-9 (eb pdf)
            [1. Mystery and detective stories. 2. Kidnapping—Fiction. 3. Maine—Fiction.]
    I. Title.
    PZ7.1.S88May 2015
    [Fic]—dc23   2015015764

Manufactured in the United States of America
1 – SB – 12/31/15

For Gabrielle, who is a natural-born storyteller, and Michael, whose inquiring mind wants to know how the world works

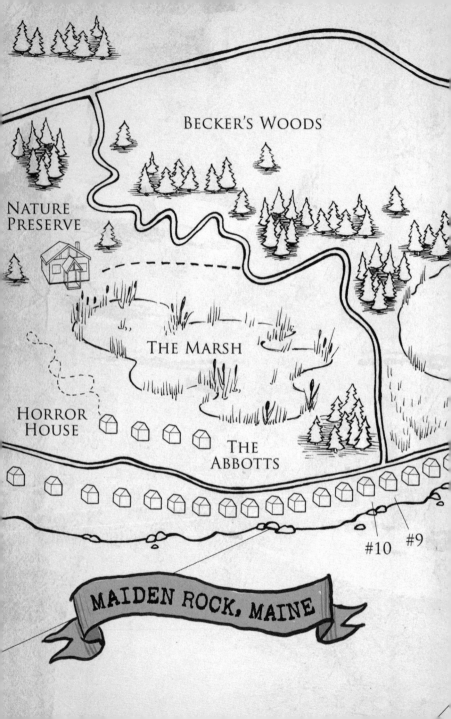

BECKER'S WOODS

NATURE PRESERVE

THE MARSH

HORROR HOUSE

THE ABBOTTS

#10   #9

MAIDEN ROCK, MAINE

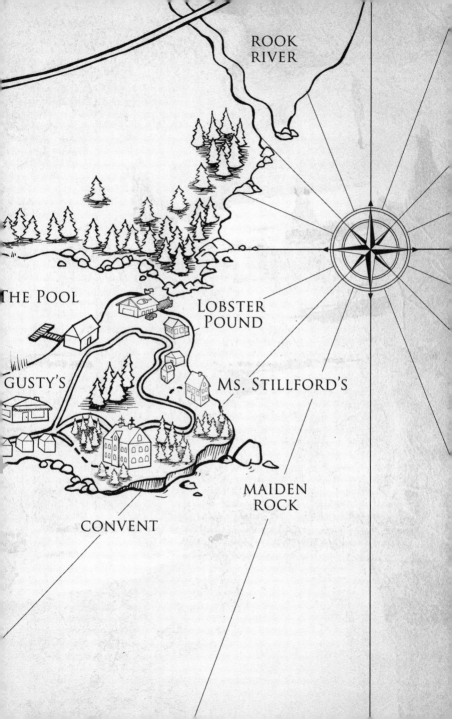

ROOK
RIVER

THE POOL

LOBSTER
POUND

GUSTY'S

MS. STILLFORD'S

MAIDEN
ROCK

CONVENT

I

Knock-knock. Knock-knock-knock. "Quinnie?"

Knock-knock. Bang, bang, bang. "Quinnette Elizabeth Boyd?"

I'm wide awake but I don't move.

"Get up. It's time to face the day."

"I don't wanna." I slide deeper under my covers. I refuse to acknowledge morning.

"Come on. Let's go school shopping. I'll take you to Rook River for new jeans and a new fleece. How about that?" Mom keeps talking but she doesn't open the door.

"No, thanks," I say with the comforter over my mouth. "You don't need new school clothes if you're homeschooled." Actually, I could use some new jeans, but I'd rather stay home and be miserable.

"You're not homeschooled," Mom says. "You're tutored. Now come on."

Who cares what you call it? "Ms. Stillford doesn't mind what I wear," I mumble.

"Well, Blythe Stillford is your teacher, and I am your mother, and I say you need some new things to perk you up. And you need notebooks and gel pens. You love that stuff. And a new cell phone case. Something nice and bright so you won't lose it. Let's go. I've got a full schedule today, so I need to be back by noon."

"My heart aches." I hadn't planned to say this out loud but I guess I did.

She sighs, and I hear her footsteps on the stairs. I know I have about ten minutes to get in the car or she'll be back up here, saying how I'm making this more dramatic than it needs to be.

* * *

"Why didn't we take your police cruiser?" I ask from the passenger seat of Mom's Real Estate SUV.

"Because this isn't official Maiden Rock sheriff business, and if we did, you'd have to ride in the back like a perp. I don't think you'd like that very much."

Sheriff and real estate lady are just two of her jobs. She's also mayor and postmaster. My mom, Margaret Boyd, is "committed to making Maiden

Rock, Maine, the jewel of the North Atlantic Coast," according to her campaign signs. The truth is, no one else would take all those jobs, and like she says, "Somebody's got to do it."

"At least we'd get good parking," I say. I'm feeling a little better, being up and out of the house. I start imagining cool new jeans with a thready tear just above my knee.

"I know you miss Zoe," she says.

Nice, Mom. And just like that, I'm back in the dumps. "Yeah, well, she doesn't miss me."

"Of course she does, Quinnie."

"I don't think so, Mom. She was smiling so big when they drove off, I thought her face would get stuck that way."

"Moving to Scotland is an adventure, Quinnie, you've got to admit that. And just think . . . for nine months, we'll have a famous crime novelist living next door to us in Zoe's house." She gives me a big smile. "*And* his daughter."

I shift to stare out the window at the endless blur of spruce and pine trees along the highway. It's a backdrop for a break-your-heart summer love story. I bury my attention in my phone. I'm halfway through my favorite episode of *Sherlock* when we take the exit to Rook River. As we drive down into town, I can see the mouth of the river dumping into the gray and white North Atlantic. I consider then reject the idea that our new novelist neighbor will look anything like Benedict Cumberbatch or even be as Maine-cool as Stephen King.

"I don't care about the famous crime writer or his stupid daughter."

"Well, you say that now. But you'll be glad you have a classmate. And who knows, maybe Mr. Philpotts will like it here so much he'll buy a place."

Right. A famous author will want to buy a house on a rocky beach north of nowhere.

"Where's the mom?" I ask.

"I don't have the full story on that yet," she says, and I can tell she's already slipped into her realtor dream-state. She gets a certain glassy-eyed look when she imagines driving buyers around and showing them houses for sale and signing the papers and collecting the commissions. I'm not making this up. If you interrupt her while she's in realtor dream-state, she'll say, "Just a second, I'm negotiating a mortgage interest rate." She believes in the power of creative visualization to make her dreams come true.

* * *

We are on our way back to Maiden Rock by 11:30 a.m. I have three bags bursting with clothes and school supplies, and I am burning to show Ms. Stillford my new Ouija board phone case; Japanese gel pens; and six-subject notebooks with colored dividers, pocket sheets, and a nine-month homework calendar.

"Let's go straight to Gusty's, Mom. Hurry."

"Don't you want to drop this stuff off at home first?"

"I want to see if Ms. Stillford's there."

"Relax, it's lunchtime. The usual gang will be there—I hope."

Gusty's is my dad's café, which was his dad's café, which was his dad's café. It's the only restaurant in town. After Labor Day, all the winter residents are expected to eat five meals a week there, as Mom says, "or the Maiden Rock economy will falter." Dad says that what she means is, "or the Boyd family finances will be in deep gull poop.'"

Mom turns left at Mile Stretch Road and drives past our house at #10, heading straight for the café. Ms. Stillford's vintage blue Volvo, with the peace sign bumper sticker, is in the parking lot.

"Look, she's here!" I pull my packages up from the backseat, whacking Mom in the head with one of them, and grab the door handle. "Sorry, Mom."

"Let me stop the car, Quinnette. She'll still be there in thirty seconds."

I wish my Mom wasn't so snippy about Ms. Stillford. They argue about everything that happens in Maiden Rock, like whether the old Abbott houses should be torn down to make way for condos (Mom's position) or preserved as historic buildings (Ms. Stillford's position). Mom says they're not arguing, they're *discussing*. Dad says, "Those two have been quibbling since Moxie was invented." Moxie is the official soda of Maine. Ms. Stillford says it tastes like root beer, and Mom says it tastes like toothpaste. But even though they go at it, Mom always says, "Blythe Stillford is the best teacher in Maine, and that's a fact."

I jump out of the car and charge through Gusty's door. Ms. Stillford is sitting at our favorite table, and Owen Loney, the lobsterman, is standing next to her. When I rush toward them, Mr. Loney backs up and bumps into a chair, almost knocking it over.

"Well, I'll be going," he says, but he doesn't walk away. He just stands there jingling his keys in his pocket.

"Oh, thank you, Owen," says Ms. Stillford. "I'd very much appreciate your fixing that screen for me." She tucks a wisp of her hair back into the thick, gray-blonde braid at the base of her neck.

Owen Loney is always hanging around Ms. Stillford. He's kind of a mopey guy. Zoe and I have heard our moms talk about how he has had the hots for Ms. Stillford for forty years. Eek!

"Okay, then. I'll be going," he says and walks away in small steps, like Ms. Stillford might call him back. She waves at him and smiles.

I'm hopping from foot to foot and willing Owen Loney to go. Go already.

"Look what I got, Ms. Stillford." I dump all my bags on the table, and the notebooks and pens spill out. Ms. Stillford catches them before they go over the edge. I flash my cell phone in front of her face. "See, it looks just like your Ouija board."

"Goodness, Quinn. What a haul!" She picks up one of the notebooks and fans through it, admiring the pocket parts and the colored tabs. Then she grabs the package of Japanese gel pens and pulls out the purple one.

"May I?" she asks me. I nod, and she flips the notebook open to the first page and writes in her perfect penmanship:

Dear Quinnie:
You are going to have so much fun in 8th grade.
I have a whirlwind of learning planned for you—so

much your head will almost explode! Ha! We will read wonderful books, write short stories, conduct exciting experiments, and learn about ancient Egypt. We'll even get to play around with pre-algebra and fractals! You are such a delightful student that you make me want to be the best teacher I can be.

I lean on the table, reading as she writes. It makes me smile until she gets to:

And wait! Let's not forget we have our new cohort, Mariella from New York, to look forward to. I wonder what she will teach us about New York and what we will teach her about Maine? There is so much fun ahead.
    Your teacher,
    Ms. Stillford

My face falls. She sees it.

"I know you miss Zoe, Quinn."

Why does everyone have to remind me that I miss Zoe?

I stand up and start putting my school supplies back in the bag.

"Show me your new clothes," she says.

So I take out my new green fleece, and Ms.

Stillford runs her fingers over the inside of the hood. "So soft," she says. "And the color is perfect for your complexion. What would you say the color is? It's like a Granny Smith apple green or maybe a pistachio green. An excellent choice for that chestnut brown hair of yours."

"Thanks," I say and flop back down into my chair.

She looks at me with her twinkly eyes and says, "How about a hug?" She doesn't wait for me to respond, which I am glad for. She just leans over and gives me a huge bear squeeze. Her beaded necklace rattles, and her lobster pin with the red stone eyes presses against my check, making a dent, but I don't care. We both miss Zoe.

"So, are we starting bright and early tomorrow morning?" she says and sits up straight.

"With our traditional blueberry pancake," I say.

"Agreed. I will meet you here at 7:00 a.m. sharp for a blueberry pancake, and eighth grade will commence."

"Mariella from New York isn't here yet," I say. I don't really care, so I'm not sure why I bring it up.

"I guess she'll just have some catching up to do, then," Ms. Stillford says, "because tomorrow at seven, it's you and me, kid."

2

"Sit down, Quinnie. Relax," Dad says.

I press my nose against the window. It's the next day, the first day of school, and Ms. Stillford is late.

"I'm going to walk outside to meet her."

"She'll be here in a minute." Dad scrapes the grill while he talks. Gusty's Café breakfast patrons have to be fed no matter what.

I stretch my neck so I can see all the way up the street. "But she said she'd be here at 7:00 a.m. sharp."

"She's probably just running late," he says.

It doesn't bother Dad one bit if people are late, or if he runs out of the day's special, or if he doesn't get his dairy delivery on time. He just makes do.

I can't wait any longer. "Back in a minute, Dad."

The door bangs shut behind me as I run out.

I head up Mile Stretch Road. A wispy fog is rolling in across the ocean on my right. It gives me my first real shiver of the season. I'm glad I brought my new pistachio green fleece. I pass the picnic area on the shore of Maiden Rock Tidal Pool on my left. We mostly just call it the Pool. It's the size of a small lake at high tide. I can see the gulls pecking at the charred remains of a Labor Day cookout at the water's edge.

I get to where Mile Stretch Road meets up with Circle Lane and stop. Ms. Stillford could be driving—or walking—from either direction. I wait at the corner for a few minutes, kicking up pebbles. I check my phone. 7:15 a.m. She is now officially fifteen minutes late.

I find her name on my contact list and tap it.

Ring. Ring. Ring. Rollover. Her musical voice reaches through the phone: "Hello. You have reached the cell phone of Blythe Stillford—"

I hang up, and as soon as I do, I decide I should have left a message.

Instead of calling back, I head toward her house out on the point. I go to the right because it's shorter, and that's the way I think she'll be coming. Yellow-tinged leaves swirl across my path. I hurry by the long, rough driveway that goes down to Our Lady of the Tides Convent. I pass the overgrown path to the high cliff above Maiden Rock, where "sailors were lured by sirens' calls, and scorned maidens threw themselves to their death"—or so the historical marker says. Rounding the bend, I expect to see Ms. Stillford huffing and puffing in my direction.

But all I see are tree limbs arching above the empty lane.

I listen for the sound of her car engine or its tires crunching on her driveway. Nothing. Only crashing surf on the rocks below, screeching gulls, and rustling branches.

Her birdhouse mailbox has a small sign tacked on its pole: *VERY PRIVATE DRIVEWAY.* I smile. That sign has caused no small debate at Gusty's, with my friend Ben's uncle, John Denby, claiming that Ms. Stillford is inviting trouble, and Owen Loney arguing that she is a "Yankee woman saying what she means."

I pull my sleeves down over my hands to warm my knuckles.

I wonder if Ms. Stillford walked the long way around Circle Lane and we are missing each other. That would be funny. No, no, it wouldn't. That would be kind of annoying. Besides, she never does that.

I scrape the gravel at the end of her driveway with a stick and feel the salty breeze across my face.

I am sure she'll appear at any second and be totally apologetic.

Waiting and bored, I flip open her mailbox.

There's mail inside. It must be yesterday's. A couple catalogs advertise autumn specials on their covers. *White Flower Farm Herbal Seeds* offers her a deal on its "Fall Color Explosion" and *Mulberry Creek Farm Herbals and Medicinals* wants her to "Explore Natural Alternatives to a Flu Shot."

Hmm.

Then it hits me that maybe she's sick—too sick to call me.

I take off down her driveway at a jog, slowing a bit at the sight of her house. It could be on the cover of *Hauntings in Ancient Maine Mansions,* one of the beat-up old books on the summer lending library shelf at Gusty's.

The windows are dark. I check my phone: 7:30. This is wrong. I wonder again about her having headed the other way and picture her walking into Gusty's and saying, "Where's Quinnie?"

The wind whips my hair, and I brush it out of my eyes.

I call Dad.

"Gusty's."

"Dad, hi. Is she there?"

"No, honey," he says. "I thought you were walking up to meet her."

"It looks like she's not home."

"Come on back here, Quinn."

"Maybe something's wrong."

"Don't make a catastrophe out of this. Come back to the café."

I hear him say good morning to Owen Loney as he hangs up.

I stand at Ms. Stillford's front door and knock.

Nothing.

Pound. Pound-pound-pound.

Nothing.

I take a deep breath. The front door is always locked, but she never locks the back door.

Something brushes my ankle. I yelp, jump back, and swat at it.

"Spiro! You gave me a heart attack!"

Ms. Stillford's skinny black cat arches its back and delivers a mournful meow. I pick him up, and he buries his face in my neck. His whiskers smell of tuna fish.

I carry him around the right side of the house. The yard opens to the sea, and the wind whistles across it, whooshing up the weathered boards and rattling the windows. A flying leaf bounces off my forehead.

The dining room drapes are open, which means she's up. I juggle Spiro and shade my eyes to look in.

Straight ahead of me, on the dining room table, lies Ms. Stillford's cell phone. I fumble my phone out of my pocket and once again scroll to her name.

Ring. Ring. Ring.

I watch as the phone's face lights up and it starts to vibrate around the tabletop.

"Hello. You have reached the cell phone of Blythe Stillford. I'm not avail—"

I bolt around the back corner of the house to the kitchen door. An eerie sound stops me cold. My brain and my ears argue over whether it was a human wail or the groan of old clapboard siding.

"Ms. Stillford?" The blustery wind swallows up my call.

As if the house has been waiting for me, the kitchen door swings open on its creaky hinges. Spiro digs his back claws into my hand as he leaps away and then dashes through the door into the kitchen. Ouch!

The back door must not have been latched, because now it bangs with each gust of wind. Okay. This happens all the time at the shore. Still, I reach into my pocket for my beach rock that goes with me everywhere.

Clutching my rock, I step into the dim early morning light of the kitchen.

A paring knife and sliced apple form a still life on

Ms. Stillford's wooden cutting board. The cut sides of the apple halves are brown. A bit of dried apple skin withers on the knife blade. A poured cup of tea has evaporated just enough to leave a stain around the inside of the rim. The bread bin lid is rolled up like it's been caught in a yawn, and a jar of peanut butter sits on the counter next to the sink—lid off. It's Ms. Stillford's favorite dinner. Dinner, not breakfast. Paused mid-making. This is so wrong.

Out of the corner of my eye, I catch Spiro disappearing into the hallway with his tail twitching. I follow him.

My imagination explodes: brain hemorrhage, concussion, broken back, crumpled body, twisted limbs. The more I picture what I might find, the more my anxiety soars and the quicker I move. The living room—not there. Her office—not there. The front hallway—not there. The pantry—not there. I pause at the stairway and yell, "Ms. Stillford?"

Nothing. I bound up the stairs.

The hallway, the bathroom—not there. I get a lump in my throat. My wonderful Ms. Stillford, my friend Ms. Stillford—not there.

I reach her bedroom door. It's closed. I choke back a sob and throw it open. There's a flutter in my chest like a hummingbird is trapped inside.

My eyes dart around the room . . . nothing.

Again. Slower. I relax my breathing and then scan, sort, identify, process.

The bed linens are tucked and tight. Her hairbrush is bristles-up on the dresser with a few silvery blond strands looped through them. A diamond ring rests in a small crystal dish. Okay, this is a little creepy. I wonder if it's the ring from her broken engagement to John Denby many years ago. Why would she keep it? The closet door is ajar and clothes rest neatly on hangers: the blue geometric print dress, the purple-and-rose silk blouse.

It all looks pretty normal. What is going on?

When I reach for my rock, I realize it's still in my hand. My fingers are sticky with blood, and the scratches Spiro gave me are seeping. When I run to the kitchen for a paper towel, I catch that I managed to smudge red along the banister.

I'm blotting my hand and planning to wipe the bannister when I look out the kitchen window and notice the garden shed. The garden shed! Maybe she's been potting or clipping or mixing or whatever she does with those herbs of hers, and she's had . . . a stroke?

I race out of the kitchen and around the side of the house. Spiro is at the shed, rubbing up against the shed door and mewing. I feel weak in the knees, but I brace myself and jerk the door open.

Nothing.

Potted flats of herbs rest under warming lights. I press the soil with my fingertips. Moist. Botany books lay open next to beakers and pipettes. Three seed packets with a picture of a purple bloom are ripped open. The text above the picture reads: *Passiflora incarnata. Common Name: Passionflower or Maypop.* Nothing unusual about this. Ms. Stillford is constantly searching for natural cures for plantar warts and who-knows-what-other grown-up sicknesses.

Maybe she blipped on school and went on errands. That's crazy. She would never do that. But if she did, then her car would be gone, right?

I peek in the old coach house Ms. Stillford uses as a garage and see it. Her car is parked in the nose-out, "ready to go" position.

My scalp prickles. With the car still in the garage, I know in my bones that something bad has happened—something super bad.

I have to find Ms. Stillford.

3

Sand and pebbles fly up into my left shoe as I race out of Ms. Stillford's yard. I don't stop. I speed down Mile Stretch Road, past Gusty's. Through the window, I see Dad and Owen Loney at the counter, drinking coffee. With every step, I organize what I will tell Mom—how I will tell Mom—so she won't think I'm overreacting. I take the steps two at a time and burst through the door to Mom's home office.

She's sitting at her Maiden Rock Real Estate desk with her feet up.

". . . a lovely four bedroom right on the beach with a fireplace." She's deep in a conversation with a possible renter. "Of course, the economy being what it is, the weekly rentals are going up four percent next summer, five in the peak weeks." She shoots me her *quiet-down* look.

"Mom," I whisper and try to catch my breath.

"Please, this is *im-por-tant*." I mouth it as clearly as I can.

She swivels her chair and turns her back to me, a view of Maiden Rock's main intersection in front of her.

I pace around the room. There are two other desks in Mom's office: the Maiden Rock mayor's desk and the Maiden Rock sheriff's desk. I sit in the sheriff's chair and jiggle my feet. I know this will get her off the phone. Unofficial people have to sit in the one of the two guest chairs.

"Thank you so much for your interest. I'll shoot you an email with the contract attached. I look forward to your joining us next summer . . . yes . . . yes . . . bye now." She spins around. "Quinnie, what's so urgent? Get out of the sheriff's chair."

I run over to her and grab her hands and say as calmly as I can, "Mom, something terrible has happened to Ms. Stillford."

Her eyebrows shoot up. "Goodness. What?"

"She's missing."

"What do you mean she's missing?"

"Missing. Gone. She didn't show up for breakfast."

Mom's shoulders relax. Not a good sign.

All of a sudden, it sounds feeble even to me, but I lay out my evidence anyway. I know that sheriffs like evidence. "I went to her house. She isn't there."

I search Mom's face for an equal level of concern and don't see it. "Her mail is still in the mailbox, the back door is wide open, and Spiro is wandering outside, but that's not all. There's food from making dinner *yesterday* on the counter in the kitchen . . . and her bed is made like maybe she didn't sleep in it, and—this is the most important thing, listen to this—her car is in the garage."

I bite my lip and wait for the horror of it to sink in.

Mom studies my face a second too long, and I know. She thinks I'm overreacting.

"Quinnie. Calm down. Sit. Over here. In the guest chair." She moves me by my shoulders. "Let's go over this again." She gives me her skeptical sheriff look. "Blythe no-showed to your breakfast with her?"

I take a deep breath. "Yes."

"Did you call her?"

"Oh my gosh, yes." I kind of lose it again. "I forgot to tell you, her cell phone is on her dining room table."

"And you know this because you, what? You went in? You went inside her house without being invited?"

"Mom, listen. She wasn't there to invite me! I knocked, but she didn't answer. I looked in the dining room window and saw the phone and then I went in the back door . . ." I pause for impact. "It was open. Like, open-open, not just unlocked. I'm telling you."

"Quinnie." Her forehead wrinkles. "Tell me you don't really believe that someone not answering their door is an invitation to go in their house."

"It was an emergency," I argue.

She gives me the one-eyebrow-arched look that tells me she's trying to decide whether this is a crisis or not. Then she lists the facts on her fingers. "You saw her cell phone on the table. You saw her bed was made. You saw some food left out on the kitchen counter. You saw her cat outside. You saw her car in the garage . . ." She raises her other hand like she'll continue on it, then drops it instead. "Everything else looked normal. Right?"

"Yes, but . . ."

Mom looks at her cell phone. "Let's see. It's now 8:12 a.m."

She gets up and puts her arm around my shoulders, and I lean away. "I don't think we're ready to file a missing persons report just yet, honey."

She pulls me close and gives me a quick hug, then slips back into her Maiden Rock Real Estate chair and shuffles papers. "We'll leave it for a while before we get all worried over nothing, okay? Oh, and

Quinnie, don't forget. Mr. Philpotts and his daughter are moving into Zoe's house on Monday, so I'd like you to put together a nice welcome basket. Maybe even a separate, special one for the daughter."

My anger flares. "I know that, Mom. You're just trying to change the subject. You don't believe me."

"I believe you. I just don't think there's an emergency quite yet. So don't take that tone with me, please."

"I hate the famous Mr. Philpotts and his New York daughter!" I feel the heat rise in my cheeks.

"The Buttermans were lucky to get a tenant for the entire winter," Mom says. "And you're lucky they have a daughter your age to replace Zoe."

"No one can replace Zoe!"

I stomp to the office doorway and spin around. "I demand to speak to the sheriff! I want to file a missing persons report."

"*Enough*, Quinn." Mom lifts her feet back up on the desk. She's already red-penciling a real estate ad when she adds, "Maybe some of those Japanese gel pens for the daughter."

I storm upstairs. Slam the door. Throw myself on the bed and pout. I know I'm not overreacting. Something is wrong, and I have to figure out what it is. Why the heck didn't I leave Ms. Stillford a message? I pull out my phone. I know it will ring on her dining room table, but I do it anyway.

This time I wait for the *beep*.

"Ms. Stillford? This is Quinnie. I . . . waited for you at Gusty's this morning, and then I went to your house and saw a bunch of things that made me wonder if you are okay. So, if you are okay, can you please call me as soon as you get this message? I told my mom that you maybe are having a problem, but she says it's too early to be concerned, but I just wanted you to—" *Beep.*

"If you are done with your message, please hang up. If you would like to listen to your message, press three. If you would like to rerecord your—"

I hang up and toss the phone across the bed. I wonder if the Ouija board on my phone case knows where she is. Probably not; even though Ms. Stillford has a Ouija board herself, she says they are just for laughs.

I hear the ocean crash and the gulls squawk, and I remember my laptop and schoolbooks are still at Gusty's.

I miss Zoe. Where are the Hebrides islands anyway? And what kind of place doesn't have Internet or cell phone service? Even if it's a 400-year-old sheep farm? And why does her dad have to study sheep parasites? She better write me a snail mail.

I want to talk to Ben, Zoe's cousin and my only other friend in Maiden Rock, but he won't get back from school in Rook River until five because of cross-country practice.

I wonder what will happen with school if something happens to Ms. Stillford . . . I stop myself thinking about that and jump up and smear some first aid cream and a bandage on my stinging palm.

I decide to go to the café and write a formal missing persons report. Mom the Sheriff can't ignore that.

I head downstairs. No sooner do I open the front door than Mom calls out, "Quinnie?"

"What?" My hand is poised on the doorknob.

"Where are you going?" The suspicious sheriff voice comes out.

"To Gusty's, to eat and get my stuff." I keep my tone level.

"Quinnie?"

"What?"

"Do not go near Blythe Stillford's house."

I don't say anything because it wasn't a question.

"Quinn?"

"What?"

"Did you hear me?"

"I heard you."

I have to be extra careful not to slam the door.

4

"Hey, honey. Didn't find Blythe yet?" Dad slides four blueberry pies into the pastry case.

"No. And I told Mom, but Mom says she's not missing."

I slip onto a stool and slouch on the counter.

"Hungry?" Dad asks.

"I guess."

"I'll pour you a pancake."

I hear the whisk in the batter, and my stomach grumbles.

Four minutes later, Dad sets the plate in front of me and leans on his elbows like what I am about to say is the most interesting thing he has ever heard. "Okay, tell me everything."

My dad is a way better listener than my mom, so I start at the beginning part, where I walked to the corner. But every time a car goes by the café, I stop and we both look out the window.

"Maybe it's a full moon," Dad says.

"What does that mean?"

"Weird things happen during a full moon. Like this morning. Owen Loney's boat engine seized up, and he couldn't run his trap lines. Never happened before—ever. See, there he goes—into Rook River, to order some odd little engine part for the *Blythe Spirit*."

We look out the window to see Owen Loney in his pickup truck, headed out of town.

I start telling Dad about how Spiro scared the heck out of me at the front door. Then Mom drives by in her sheriff's cruiser, going the other way, from our house toward the point. My hopes soar—maybe she's going to Ms. Stillford's. Dad sees me sit up.

"Don't get excited. She's just going to the post office," he says. "She called before you got here."

Mom talks to Dad ten times a day. They talk about everything: what's going on in Maiden Rock, what I'm doing, strange boats that come into the Pool, strange cars in town, summer people problems, rental house issues, late trash pickup, you name it. They talk.

Then I tell him how Spiro smelled like tuna fish, and I get all the way to the part of my story where

Ms. Stillford's car is in the garage when Sister Rosie and Sister Ethel whiz by in their white convent van.

"Where are they going?" I ask Dad. He seems to know where everyone is headed.

"Only God knows that, Quinnie. Those two don't keep me updated on their comings and goings." He laughs. "But they sure get around. Maybe they're going to church in Rook River."

When I was born, twenty-five nuns lived at Our Lady of the Tides. One after the other, they got old and died. There's a row of little white crosses at the cemetery in Rook River that say *OLT* and the date. No names. I think that's wrong. Even if you marry Jesus and all, you should have your real name on your grave. Sister Rosie and Sister Ethel are the only two left.

"It's lucky for the sisters that Mom is at the post office," I say.

"Yep." He picks a piece of pancake off my plate with his fingers and pops it in his mouth.

He smiles and pours himself a cup of coffee and sits down on the stool next to me. We both know that speeding in Maiden Rock makes Mom cranky. Speeding, not recycling, and beer on the beach are the top three infractions that will get you on Sheriff Boyd's most-wanted list.

"I agree that this thing with Blythe is strange, Quinnie. It doesn't make sense that she'd not show up for breakfast with you *and* her car'd be in her garage like that."

"I *know!*" Finally. Someone else sees the problem.

"Maybe she walked the other way and slipped and fell," he offers. "But your mother just drove that way, so if Blythe took a spill on the road, she'd see her for sure and she'd already be driving back here with her flashers on."

"But what about the apple, Dad? The brown apple?"

He gives it further consideration, then looks me in the eye and says, "It's just an apple, honey. I've been known to leave a bread bag open overnight."

Since Dad's willing to listen to everything I have to say, I go through it all again while he cleans up the dishes, makes the chowder, and picks the lobster meat out of its shells. But I can tell he isn't worried.

A black Escalade turns into the parking lot and angles in too close to the front door. Dad squints to check it out. Four grungy characters get out of the car and crowd through the door. Dad says "full moon" under his breath. He wipes the already-clean counter over and over and watches them.

There are two guys and two girls. At first I can't stop looking at the girl with the pink hair. The swoop of it rivals a Smurf's head. Then my eyes shift to the other girl. Mom always says don't stare, but the other girl, the one with the blue and purple hair, is completely stare-worthy. All I can think is, maybe one of them is Lady Gaga. I know that is probably not possible, since Lady Gaga would not be with either of these two guys or here in Maiden Rock.

The big guy has a ponytail, tattoos, and a fringed leather jacket. The small guy has almost no hair and a mustache. He has plenty of tattoos, too, and a chunky chain with a big cross around his neck.

Dad bumps my arm, and I realized my mouth is open. I snap it shut.

I am getting ready to be nervous about them and I can tell Dad is too, when they start talking and laughing.

"This place looks awesome, Trinka," the blue-haired girl says.

"Totally authentic, Bin," says the pink-haired girl.

"I bet we can score some serious chowder," says the big guy. He looks around, then nods at Dad.

"Any table," Dad says but points to the one he can watch from the kitchen.

They scrape back the chairs and make a big deal

about who's going to sit where. The big guy picks his chair first. Then the rest of them settle down like a flock of gulls.

Dad walks over with four glasses of water and menus.

I see Mom's cruiser come down Mile Stretch Road at a normal speed, then slow down and crawl by the café. She stops but doesn't pull in the parking lot. The next thing I hear is Dad's cell phone going off.

I escape to my table, open my laptop to work on my missing persons report, and watch from behind it. So much is happening, I can't wait for Ben to get back to Maiden Rock after school. I send him a text message that says: *Ms. Stillford missing. MR invaded by tattooed rockers.*

5

The rockers from the Escalade order a ridiculous amount of food, which has Dad smiling from ear to ear. Mom must have been convinced that all was well, because she's taken off for who knows where— probably to deliver the mail. Dad's been running back and forth to the rocker table with second bowls of chowder and taking orders from some regulars who've come in for lunch. The regulars give the rockers hard looks.

I take in reactions around the café, which are mostly a lot of eyebrow talk. I look from table to table until something on the floor in the corner catches my eye. When I move my head, it sparkles in the light. I get up and walk over to it.

Ms. Stillford's lobster pin! The one she wore yesterday. The one with ruby eyes and gold-tipped claws. I touch my cheek where it had pressed against me.

She must have lost it yesterday at lunchtime, when I saw her, because she wasn't here last night for dinner. At dinnertime, she was at home, cutting an apple and planning to eat a peanut butter sandwich.

I set the pin on the table next to my computer, open a blank document, and make a list of everything I can remember: I saw her here at Gusty's yesterday at noon. She was wearing her lobster pin. This morning, she missed the first day of school. There's a cut brown apple on her counter, which must have been from last night's dinner. Her mail from yesterday is still in her mailbox. Her bed is made like she didn't sleep in it. The cat smells of tuna fish, like he's been fed recently. Her phone is on the dining room table. The plants in the shed have been watered. Her car is in the garage.

I know I'm "obsessing," as Mom calls it—going over something again and again—but it calms me to write down everything I can remember. If Ms. Stillford doesn't show up by dinnertime, I'll print it out and give it to Mom as part of my official missing persons report. If Ms. Stillford shows up, I'll let her read it. I imagine her laughing and saying, "Oh, my stars. I had no idea I caused such a stir. I'm so sorry. I got so busy thinking about cinnamon from Zanzibar that I went to the spice shop and forgot about school completely. So, so sorry."

I keep looking at my phone, hoping it will play Patsy Cline's "Crazy." That's the ringtone Ms. Stillford uses on her phone, so I programmed it in my phone for when she calls me. Ben says it makes his ears bleed to listen to country—even ringtones. I've told him ten times that not everyone wants to listen to hip-hop.

I can't wait for him to show up. My phone vibrates with Ben's thoughtful response to my horrific news: *Shut up!*

＊ ＊ ＊

He doesn't get to the café until 5:30 p.m. By that time, I've been back and forth between home and the café three times, and the rockers have come back for another Gusty's Down East meal.

"Did she say you couldn't go *in* the house, *near* the house, or *to* the house?" Ben asks. He's thrown his schoolbooks next to mine on the table.

"I can't remember exactly." I think back to when I had my hand on the doorknob and Mom was warning me. "I think she said *to* the house, which really means *in* the house, right?"

Ben looks at the rockers, who are sitting at the same table as before.

"They're goofy for Gusty's," I say. "They were here for lunch and now they're here for dinner. They ate all the chowder, so I hope you want a BLT."

This time, the rockers are gorging on a lobster fries platter and Gusty burgers. They lick their fingers, smack their lips, and ooh and ahh over every lemony, buttery bite. They already ate one whole blueberry pie at lunch and told Dad to save them another one for dinner. Dad's hovering over them with coffee refills like they might be restaurant critics in disguise.

"I'd kinda go for that blue-haired girl," Ben says and gives me a *ya know* nod.

"Forget them. Pay attention. I'm telling you about Ms. Stillford."

Ben licks his thumb and wipes a smudge of dirt off the top of his running shoe. His wet hair curls at the nape of his neck. Cross country. He runs every day after school until the snow's too thick to slog through. After his post-practice shower, he comes straight here, and I worry that he's going to catch pneumonia.

But not as much as I am worrying about Blythe Stillford right now.

"Maybe she was abducted," he says.

"I think so too!" I squeal. "But by who?"

"I don't know. Aliens. They kidnap humans and subject them to complex physical and psychological testing."

"*Puh-leez!* Be serious."

"I am serious. This guy, Antonio Boas, was abducted in the 1950s, and nobody's been able to prove he wasn't, and scientists studied the snot out of him."

I slap his arm. "So, do you want to walk to her house with me?" I ask.

"Sure."

"We won't go in. We'll just walk by it." I convince myself that this is in compliance with whatever Mom said.

"Let's go. I'm ready." He stands up, all long legs and arms, and digs his hands into his hoodie pockets.

"Quinnie?" Dad calls from the kitchen. "Where're you guys going?" I know immediately by his tone that Mom's told him about her order.

"We're just going to walk around Circle Lane. Just to check. That's all." I feel a little like I am daring him to stop me.

He hesitates for a second and then his shoulders relax. "Oh, that's fine. Don't go in the house—or in the yard. Okay, Quinnie?"

I zip up my fleece so hard I catch the bandage on my palm. *Ouch.* "Okay." He's still looking at me. "*Okay!*" I say.

"And don't be gone long." He looks at the rocker gang, then over to my and Ben's computers and schoolbooks, and mouths, "I'll watch your table."

The rockers look older than they did this afternoon, like maybe in their thirties or even older. And they look richer, maybe like real rock stars. The big guy raises his inked arm to us as we pass their table. He points his finger at Ben, and I notice he's wearing a chunky ring on his pointer finger. A skull ring. Now I have a name for him: Skullfinger.

"Yo, man," Skullfinger says to Ben. "We're headed for Rook River. You know it?"

"It's the next town up the coast," Ben says. "On the other side of the channel, and on the other side of the river."

The whole rocker table thinks this is interesting. The blue-haired girl is combing her hair with her black fingernails.

"So how do you get there from here?" Skullfinger says and licks butter off the side of his hand.

"You've got to go back out to the main road," Ben says.

"Can't drive up this way?" Skullfinger asks, jerking his thumb up Mile Stretch Road.

"Nope," I say. "It's a peninsula."

Skullfinger pulls out his phone, taps Google Maps about ten times and squints. "That's stupid. I figured there'd be, like, bridges or something."

I decide that I do not like these people even though they may be rock stars and even though they bought a ton of food.

"You got, like, a lobster store in this town?" Skullfinger asks. His eyes are like black glass.

"Lobster *pound*," I say. I want to look at Ben like *sheesh*, but I'm a little afraid to.

The blue-haired girl bumps Skullfinger with her elbow. "Hey, what are you gonna do with lobsters?"

His eyes flash, and he turns snarly. He pokes his finger in her face. "Shut up, Bin. Nobody asked you. Maybe I'll bring 'em back here and have this Gusty guy cook 'em up. You like the cooking all right, don't ya? You can't stop stuffing your face."

Tension sparks all over the room, and Ben and I are out the door in a nanosecond. The next thing I know, we're in the parking lot, looking back in through the window.

"Those guys are drunk," Ben says.

"Or something," I say. "You think we should leave Dad alone with them?"

But before we can worry about that too much, Ben's Uncle John drives up and gets out of his pickup. "Where're you two going? Have you had dinner, Ben?" he asks.

We look at each other. Why does everyone want to know where we're going all the time?

Ben's Uncle John is so strict that he's kind of mean to Ben, making rules and giving him limits all the time. Ben's parents died in a car accident when he was two. Dad says Ben popped out of the crash strapped in his car seat, without a scratch on him. Ever since then, his uncle has been his guardian. Mom says John doesn't know how to be a parent but he does the best he can.

"We're walking out to the point and back," Ben says. "I have to work out my hamstrings a little more." He shakes his leg like it has a cramp. "I'll eat when I get back. Is that okay?"

His uncle looks at his watch. "No more than thirty minutes."

"There's no chowder left," I say. "And I think Dad could use some company."

John Denby looks through the window at the rockers, then at the Escalade.

"Got it," he says, walks into Gusty's, and calls to Dad, "Hey, Gus. I hope you got some chowder left."

I look at the Escalade and its dark tinted windows, and I have a crazy thought. What if Ms. Stillford is tied up in the back of that car?

6

"I'd stay away from that thing if I were you," Ben says as I walk toward the black monstrosity. "It probably has an alarm."

"What if Ms. Stillford is in there?" I ask.

"What possible reason could those guys have for kidnapping Ms. Stillford?"

I know a criminal has to have a motive. I know that from being a sheriff's daughter. A criminal needs motive, means, and opportunity. I look back through the window at the rockers. Trinka is fixing her lipstick. Bin is picking her teeth with her fingernail. The guy with *Stevie* tattooed on his arm is draining a cup of coffee. Skullfinger is staring blankly and chewing. Ben's right. These goofballs have less reason to kidnap Ms. Stillford than an alien would.

We walk toward the point. It's not even six o'clock, and the sun is fading.

Maiden Rock is at its worst in the week right after Labor Day. The beach houses look tired. From the road, you only see the backs of them. Back doors. Garage doors. Garbage bins overflowing with the summer people's last loads of trash. Only the Woodsons' place has fresh white paint. The rest of the houses are peeling like pale skin after a sunburn.

I check my phone. No calls.

I reach into my pocket and touch my rock.

I open my mouth, but the words don't come out right away.

"I'm scared, Ben."

Then this boy I have known my whole life, who treats me like a cousin, but who I think I might want to marry when I grow up, does the sweetest thing. He grabs me around the neck like he's applying a wrestling hold and says, "Aw, Q. It'll be okay."

I feel a flush of heat on my face and I have a little hope that he's right.

"Where do you think she is?" I ask him.

"It's only, like, since this morning, right?"

"Yeah, but it's the first day of school." I stop and grab his arm. "If you didn't talk to your uncle all day, and he didn't show up to pick you up at school, you'd worry, right?"

He pauses for a second. "Yeah, I guess so."

We walk on in silence.

"Look along the side of the road," I say.

"Why?"

"Because she may have tripped and hit her head or something and, I don't know, rolled in the bushes."

He looks at me like I'm dumb, which I hate. "If she fell on Mile Stretch Road or Circle Lane, she'd have to roll twenty feet to be out of sight."

Fine. The Ben I heart is gone, and Mr. Know-It-All is back. I say *heart* because I am not ready to say the L-word. Maybe Zoe is right. She says maybe I only heart him because he's the only boy in town my age. But I don't think so. There are boys around all summer long, every summer. There are city boys, rich boys, nice boys, fun boys, boys who any girl would call cute. Yet I *heart* Ben, even though he is clueless . . . and even though sometimes he really makes me mad. Like right at this very moment, when he treats me like I'm dumb and takes off jogging.

"Where are you going?" I call after him.

"To look around."

"We can't go in."

"No. *You* can't go in."

"Don't touch anything!" I yell. "It could be evidence!"

I start running after him. I run past the locked and chained Maiden Rock Yacht Club, past Loney's Lobster Pound ("All Sales Final"), by the boarded-up Miss Wickham's Bed & Breakfast, by the closed-for-the-winter Bradford's Grocery, past the practically dollhouse-sized post office. I'm panting when I reach Ms. Stillford's driveway. He's not there.

"Ben!"

I listen intently but hear only gull calls and thrashing branches. It's getting colder. I pull up my hood and scoop in hair that by now looks like a tangled ball of twine.

"Bennnnn!" I yell into the wind.

I pace at the entrance to Ms. Stillford's driveway. What is he doing? What is he finding? He knows how much I hate waiting.

Back and forth. Back and forth.

Zzzzzt. Zzzzzt. My phone vibrates in my pocket then bursts into "Get Low," one of Ben's all-time favorites—a classic, according to him.

"Ben! Where are you?"

"Jeez, you're welcome." I hear the wind blowing through his phone.

"Why? What?"

"I crawled out over the edge of the cliff to see if she fell off and cracked her head on the rocks," Ben says.

"What! That's crazy unsafe!"

"Yeah, well, no dead Ms. Stillford down there."

It sounds like he's running, and then the phone goes dead. I hate this. What's happening now? I just about decide to go after him when he jogs out of the shadows.

His knees and shins are smudged gray-brown. He brushes dirt off his shoes.

Anger and relief swirl inside me, but all that comes out is, "Were there any lights on in her house?"

"Nah, it was dark," he says. "I think. But I mostly checked the cliff."

Really? I want to scream that the whole purpose of him going down there was to check out the house, but I tell myself to be glad he eliminated the most *unlikely* possibility—that she fell. I'm thinking I should go down the driveway myself to see if there is any sign she's at home.

Now Ben's jumping around like he's cold.

"I'm starving," he says.

"Can you wait two seconds?"

"I already told you she didn't go over the cliff."

"Ben!"

Sometimes I do not understand how his mind works.

"My uncle's gonna wonder where we are."

I stare down Ms. Stillford's driveway.

"Uh oh." Ben stands still and looks over my shoulder.

I spin around. The sheriff's cruiser crunches gravel as it approaches. It rolls up to us, flashers on, and stops. I'd like to dive into the bushes, but Mom's obviously seen me, so I stand up straight and take a deep breath. The driver's window powers down, and she locks eyes with me.

Nobody says anything until I crack. "I didn't go past the mailbox."

She shifts her gaze to Ben. "Get in the backseat. Both of you."

Riding in the back of the police cruiser, where Mom puts criminals and suspects, is humiliating even in an empty town.

She doesn't give me the how-disappointed-I-am lecture. But I know by the look in her eyes in the rearview mirror. From across the chain-mesh seat divider, she suspects me of pressuring Ben into going to the house. I decide this is not a good time to bring up my plan to file an official missing persons report.

* * *

That night, I stare out my bedroom window. I can see whitecaps even at night, with the help of the moonlight and the lights from the convent up the beach. I wait for the whispering of the surf to offer me an explanation for what's happening. I get nothing. When I was little and stayed overnight at Ms. Stillford's, sleeping in the blue guest room that faced the ocean, she would put her finger to her lips and say, "Listen, Quinnie. It's like the ocean is saying *shssssh* . . . It's telling us to go to sleep."

But I can't go to sleep tonight. I open my computer and add to my list of facts: *Didn't fall off, jump off, or get pushed off the Maiden Rock cliff.*

Then I decide my report needs an opening statement. I look up "missing persons reports" on the Internet, and using one as a model, I start typing:

Blythe Stillford, age 60, of Maiden Rock failed to appear for a breakfast meeting on Friday morning, September 12th, at Gusty's Café. A visit to her residence showed signs of suspicious activity.

I practice the rule that Ms. Stillford taught me of letting it rest for a couple hours or overnight, so I leave the report as a draft and plan to get up really early tomorrow. If she hasn't called, I'll finalize it. But before I even log out of the computer, I read through the whole thing again, and soon I am sniffing and wiping my nose on my pajama top. I try to sleep, but her face keeps pushing to the front of my mind. I keep saying over and over like a chant, "Ms. Stillford, please be safe. Ms. Stillford, please be safe. Ms. Stillford, please be safe."

7

My eyes pop open at 5:35 a.m. the next morning. I have a mark on my cheek from falling asleep on my phone—which I check immediately. No messages.

I know Dad is already rolling out cinnamon buns at the café by now, but Mom is still in bed snoring like a walrus—that's how Dad describes it. If Ms. Stillford heard me repeat this, she'd say, "Interesting. I wonder if walruses actually snore. Quinnie?" And I'd research it on the Internet and tell her they do, and she'd say. "Fascinating. Thank you for that, my dear."

I dress and hurry down to the kitchen to make toast with apple butter and a slice of cheddar. Five minutes later, I am standing at Mom's side of the bed with the plate and a napkin. She doesn't move, so I lower the plate to her nose. One eyelid opens.

Her lips barely move. "I guess this means you haven't heard from Blythe?"

"Correct." I wave the plate. "Just like you like it."

She groans. "It's Saturday morning."

"Yes, it is." I use her arguing-with-me-will-do-no-good voice.

She flips back the covers, sits up, and yawns. I don't know if it's because she's rested or weary. I don't care which.

I continue calmly. "We are going to Ms. Stillford's to check on her."

Mom rubs the bedhead out of her hair.

"Fine," she says and takes the plate from me. The last thing I see before the bathroom door shuts behind her is her jaw working on a bite of toast. Mom's willingness to do this actually gets me more worried.

I force myself to sit still as I wait in the car.

Through the big picture window in Mom's office, I watch her switch on the light and lean over her real estate desk. I know she's digging in the drawer that has all the Maiden Rock keys. Before long, she climbs into the car with Ms. Stillford's house key in her hand.

We head toward Gusty's. I know Mom needs Dad's morning blend.

"I'll go in and get your coffee," I offer.

"We'll both go in."

"Do you want to get a cinnamon bun?" I ask. I am sure this makes me sound reasonable and not panicky.

"Maybe. Are you hungry?"

"No." No. No. No. I just want to get going.

We pull into Gusty's parking lot. Inside, John Denby is at the counter warming his hands around a mug. Dad has a large pan of buns on the counter. He wields two forks as he pulls the buns apart and moves each one onto a plate. Hot, sticky icing strands trail across the counter.

John Denby turns to Mom as we walk in and says, "You gals going up to Blythe's?"

Dad puts a carryout cup of coffee and a bun in front of Mom and winks at me.

Mom nods at John Denby and splashes cream into her coffee. "Just a quick check to satisfy Quinnie."

I hate it when she does this—says something to somebody else that is really a message to me.

"Want me to come along?" John Denby asks.

Mom says, "Nah, I got this." She rips off a piece of cinnamon bun and lifts it to her mouth. Some brown sugary goo gets on her chin and she grabs a paper napkin from the holder. The goo drops onto her favorite yellow sweater before she can nab it. Oh, no.

"Darn it!" She dips the napkin in the water glass and blots the spot.

"Remember the time she went on the Save the Whales protest and forgot to tell anybody?" John

Denby asks, but it's not really a question. "She's a flighty one."

"You can say that again," says Mom. I watch the blot get bigger as she fusses.

I don't remember anything about saving the whales. "What protest?" I ask, but they ignore me.

This is making me crazy, but if I want Mom to go with me to Ms. Stillford's and be serious about it, I have to keep my mouth shut. I can't yell that John Denby always talks down Ms. Stillford when she's not around because he has hurt feelings that won't go away because she broke their engagement a hundred years ago. And I can't yell that Mom always bashes on Ms. Stillford when she's not around because they disagree about what's good for Maiden Rock. So I'm quiet. I look at my phone. It's 7:05, and I wonder if my little Ouija board knows if Ms. Stillford is back home safe and sound.

I make a perfectly calm effort to get Mom moving.

"I'll wait for you outside, Mom," I say.

"OK. I'll be right there," she says.

But it's 7:27 before she comes out. I know this because I look at my phone every minute, and because that's when the incident happens with the sisters.

Headlights pop out of the convent driveway. Mom sees them and runs to our car and pulls out a monster-sized flashlight and positions herself at the side of the road. The sister's van barrels toward her. Mom raises her arm and waves the light in a broad arc to flag them down. The van brakes screech. The sisters skid sideways, directly at Mom. I scream. Tires squeal. The van driver regains control and brings it to a rocking halt.

I look at Mom. Her eyebrows have joined into that scary unibrow. Her cup is on the ground by our car, but most of the coffee has soaked into her sweater, near the grease blot. It's starting to look like she's wearing leopard print.

Mom takes her time walking to the driver's window. She taps the window three times with the flashlight. I can see two faces in old-fashioned nun's habits as the window powers down. The sisters have worn wimples for as long as I've known them, even though most nuns dress like normal people now.

"Sister Rosie." Mom pauses a moment to see if either of the nuns says anything. "Where is the fire?" The words go into the van like little puffs of dragon breath.

Sister Rosie, the driver, looks as small as a large woman can look.

"I know, dear. I'm so sorry. I didn't know anyone was out this early."

Whoa. I know right away this is the worst answer ever. Even I wouldn't make this mistake.

"Really, Sister? You were speeding because you didn't think anyone was around?"

"Well, I didn't mean it like that, dear."

"I don't know what to say, Sister. You speed when there are no people around, and you speed when there are people around. I'm not seeing any difference."

"I know, dear. I'm so sorry. Give me a ticket. Go ahead."

Mom takes a step backwards and bounces her flashlight against her leg. "Well, I haven't heard that one before," she says. She stares at the drainpipe on Gusty's roof like she's trying to remember something, but I know that look. She's trying to calm down.

"I guess it's in God's hands," says Sister Rosie.

Uh oh, another wrong answer. I could tell that Sister Rosie was kidding, but Mom does not look like she's in the mood for a joke.

"I don't know about God's hands, Sister. But I'm giving you a final warning." Mom takes a step toward the van and leans over to look Sister Rosie in the eye. "If I catch you speeding again, you *will* get a ticket, and if you keep getting tickets, you *will* lose your license. And I don't think that is what God expects from you. And while we're at it, how's the separating for recycling going?"

Sister Ethel, who's sitting in the passenger seat, leans over and whispers to Sister Rosie behind a cupped hand. When she's done, Sister Rosie sits up straight.

"Thank you, dear. Bless you, dear," says Sister Rosie like she's following instructions from Sister Ethel. "You don't need to worry. From now on, I will be a model driver. And yes, we'll separate the paper and the glass. We know."

Mom stands back and watches as Sister Rosie throws the van in gear and accelerates at the speed of a tortoise.

At that rate, I imagine they will get to Rook River tomorrow.

Mom turns to me. "Where are they going at this hour anyway?"

That is a sheriff kind of question. Where would these two nuns be going at 7:30 on a Saturday morning?

"Probably the Walmart in Rook River," I say.

"I guess even nuns buy toilet paper in bulk," Mom mutters.

8

As we pull into Ms. Stillford's yard, the sun popping up over the ocean makes me squint. I run to the front door ahead of Mom. She takes her time getting out of the car. Spiro bolts from the woods, his back arched like a Halloween cat, and hops sideways toward me. I lean down and pick him up. The tuna fish smell still clings to his whiskers.

Mom knocks on the front door—normal at first, then harder.

"The back door's unlocked, Mom."

"That's not the protocol, Quinnette."

I rub Spiro's ear, and he pushes his head into the palm of my hand, which is still tender. I loosen my grip on him and carefully set him down.

Mom steps back and digs for the key in her pocket. It falls to the ground, and I scoop it up and hand it to her. She tells me to stop hovering.

Mom turns the house key in the brass lock and puts her shoulder into the door. Spiro shoots past us, through the paneled entryway and the coat closet, down the hall, and up the stairs.

"Blythe?" Mom calls. She opens the coat closet door and looks up and down.

There's a row of suitcases on the floor of the closet, small, medium, and large. The spot for Ms. Stillford's extra-large suitcase is empty. The coats on the hanging bar have been separated and pushed aside. Two empty hangers rock in the middle of the bar.

Mom turns and looks at me. "Looks like a suitcase and a couple coats are gone." It sounds half like an accusation and half like a confirmation.

"I didn't look in here yesterday," I admit. But that doesn't mean she wasn't kidnapped . . . Except people don't pack for a kidnapping.

We move into the living room. Mom stands in the middle and slowly turns in a circle. I do the same. Then she walks toward the dining room. I pull out my phone and call Ms. Stillford's number. In my ear, I hear it ring then roll to voice mail. In the dining room, I hear . . . nothing.

I walk toward the dining room table. "Her phone's gone!"

"I thought you said it was on the dining room table?"

"It *was*, Mom. It was right there on the table yesterday morning."

I point to the spot where it had lit up when I called it.

Mom walks around the dining room table and leans down to look across the surface, as if a new angle will show a mark where the phone had been.

"Call it again," she says.

I dial, get the voice mail, and hand my phone to her.

Mom clears her throat.

"Blythe, this is Margaret, calling on Quinnie's phone. We're at your house because we were a little concerned that you missed breakfast yesterday and we haven't heard from you. Please call me when you get this message and let us know all is well."

She presses *END* and hands it back to me.

She moves on to Ms. Stillford's office. It's decorated in what Ms. Stillford calls microcosm-of-her-brain style. An Acadia National Park cup stuffed with pencils and pens, a stapler, a dish of rainbow paper clips, a little Maine souvenir burlap pillow stuffed with balsam needles, tabbed notebooks, half of a chocolate bar, a black felt monkey with a pink face, a box of something called Sanctity Tea. Open books are stacked next to the computer. Ms. Stillford always has books piled up that way—like she's in the middle of researching something. I look at the titles: *The Botany of Desire: A Plant's-Eye View of the World, Manual of Flowering Plants, Red Lily Guide to Hydroponic Gardening.*

The computer screen is dark, but the little green light glows. Another thing I didn't notice yesterday.

"The computer's on, Mom."

Mom takes a tissue out of her pocket, wraps it around her finger, and presses the space bar. The monitor wakes up to a screen about hydroponic gardening. There are two tabs at the top of the screen. One tab says *Common Name Passionflower or Maypop.* The other says *Quinnie Boyd.* Mom clicks on the Quinnie Boyd tab. It's the short story that I sent Ms. Stillford last week about things in my bureau drawer. She's in the middle of writing comments on it using Track Changes. Mom's eyes scan the page.

"Cha-cha-cha polka-dot panties?" She looks at me with wide eyes.

"It's a story, Mom. It's supposed to be funny."

"*Oh*-kay."

She walks away from the computer but says, "Don't touch it. Just leave it on. Let it go back to sleep."

She heads into the kitchen. I hurry to get ahead of her. "Look at the apple, Mom."

"What apple?"

"Hey! It's gone." The knife is gone too. And the bread bin is closed.

I open the cabinet under the sink and look in the trash basket. The browned apple halves are at the bottom. Next, I run to the cupboard and yank it open. There it is. "See, there's the peanut butter jar. The lid's on."

Now Mom is looking at me like I'm crazy.

"I see it." She spins and gives the kitchen another scan. "Looks like it's clean and ready for Blythe to go on a trip."

She walks out of the kitchen toward the stairs, and I hear her gasp.

"Stay back, Quinn."

I lick my lips and gulp.

"There's blood on the banister."

I rush up behind her and see the red smear from my cat scratches.

"Wait, Mom. That's my blood."

"Don't be silly."

She takes her phone out of her pocket.

"No! Wait a minute. It *is* my blood."

I show her my hand with the bandage and stand

on the steps and demonstrate where I grabbed the banister. She takes my hand and turns it over to see the palm.

"How did this happen?"

"Spiro. I was holding him and jumped out of my hands."

"When?"

"Yesterday morning."

"Oh, Quinnie. Did you put antibiotic cream on it?"

"Uh huh."

"You wait here. I'm going to take a sweep upstairs." As she disappears around the bend in the stairway, she yells, "Don't touch anything."

I yell back, "Should I wipe off the banister?

I can't hear her answer so I run up after her.

When I see the bedroom I freeze.

The closet door gapes open. Bare hangers crowd together where dresses hung neatly yesterday. A scarf is sticking out of the top bureau drawer. The hair-brush is gone!

I walk through the bedroom with my mouth hanging open. In the bathroom, Ms. Stillford's medicine cabinet door is ajar, and there are empty spots where pill containers had been. The toothbrush is gone!

"Mom, someone has been here."

"Yes, Quinnie. It looks like someone named Blythe Stillford has been here," she says. "In her house, packing for a trip, cleaning up, and leaving. Probably for the weekend."

A million images flash through my mind. Did she leave and then come back? Did she come back and then go away again?

"Ms. Stillford? Are you here?" I scream.

"Calm down, Quinnie. Let's get out of Blythe's house. She's obviously not here."

"But what about her phone? Why didn't she call me back? Why didn't she answer it? Why didn't she come to breakfast? What about the first day of school?"

"I agree with you about that. I intend to have a serious talk with her about starting school on time."

I might be a little mad at Ms. Stillford now. It looks like she grabbed some clothes, cleaned up her kitchen in a big hurry, then took off again. *And* she has her phone *and* she has my messages *and* she knows how worried I am *and* she hasn't called me.

"The car." I pull at Mom's sleeve. "Let's see if it's still here."

I run to the garage fully expecting her car to be gone. But there sits the blue Volvo, still poised for action.

"Mom, she wouldn't come back and pack a suitcase and walk away. She had to be with someone. Or maybe someone else was here."

"Let's go, Quinn." Mom sounds irritated. "This is looking more like a case of her being inconsiderate than being kidnapped."

"No, wait. I know something is wrong," I say.

Mom rubs her temples with her fingertips. "Sometimes you are the most measured, logical, intelligent girl, and sometimes you are, well, overly excitable."

"But the car?" My voice comes out feeble and shaky.

"She could have been picked up."

"But the phone?"

"Maybe she forgot her charger."

Then for some crazy reason, I flash on a possible explanation. I know that saying it will probably stir up a lot of trouble, but I have to make a choice: to avoid Mom's anger or to save Ms. Stillford.

"Mom. Listen to me . . . I think maybe Owen Loney kidnapped Ms. Stillford."

"What?" Her voice is shaky, soft, halting.

"You know how he always hangs around her, all puppy-dog faced, and he's always offering to give her rides and fix her house, and you and Zoe's mom say he's got the hots for her—"

The next thing I know, Mom grabs my upper arm and practically pulls me off my feet toward the car. She doesn't look at me while she talks. "Quinnette, you don't go around accusing honest, hardworking people of horrific felonies. Have you lost your senses? Who are you?"

"Ouch, Mom! That hurts." I try to jerk my arm away, but she tightens her grip and steers me into the backseat of her car.

Mom's hands squeeze the steering wheel as she drives. She keeps her eyes straight ahead. By the time we reach our house, I have a bucket of tears ready to gush, but they won't come.

Mom parks but doesn't get out of the car.

"Go in the house, Quinnette. I'm going back to Gusty's and then to Rook River for groceries. Do not leave the house while I'm gone. Are we clear?"

I jump out of the car, slam the door, and stomp up the steps.

Mom sticks her head out of the car window. "Are we clear?"

I spin around, lift my chin, and yell, "Oh yeah? Well, who are you? You're supposed to be the sheriff. You're supposed to care about the victim. You're a mother. You're supposed to care about your daughter. I don't know who you are either!"

"And Quinnie . . . you're not ordering *unusual* underwear online, are you?"

"No, Mom. It's a *story*. I made it up. It's called fiction. Don't you know that?"

Her face is as tight as a stiff sail. "All I know is that you better not be ordering some kind of cha-cha pants online, whatever those are."

9

I sit on the floor of my room for a long time, waiting for tears to flow, but they don't. I'm sure Mom's fuming, and I should feel worse than I do about yelling at her that way, but this is not about us right now. It's about Ms. Stillford. Her safety is the most important thing.

I pull my phone out of my pocket and scroll to *Ben*. Once the phone connects us, I hear a rustle of wind against the speaker.

"Hey," Ben says.

"Where are you?"

"I'm on a run."

"Where?"

"By the Abbotts."

"Can you come to my house?" I ask.

"Are you allowed visitors?"

"Oh, you heard. Is she at Gusty's, telling everybody?"

66

"She told my uncle that you're home so you can *think a few things over*, and he called and told me not to bother you. Small town, remember?"

"Ugh."

"So spill."

"If you come here," I say, "I'll spill it all and feed you too."

Food usually gets Ben's complete attention. So I'm still pulling things out of the refrigerator when he runs up from the beach side of the house and bangs through the kitchen door, bringing the smell of salt air with him.

A loaf of Dutch crust bread toasted medium brown and buttered, a third of a pound of sliced Havarti cheese, a jar of bread-and-butter pickles, three oranges, half a package of Oreos, and a quart of milk later, he burps. Then he reaches for a stale cinnamon bun in a baggie on the counter.

"And you think it's Owen Loney because . . . he wasn't out on his trap lines yesterday morning?" Ben asks between bites.

"He had opportunity. Like my mom says, 'Suspects have to have opportunity.'"

"Aliens have opportunity."

"Shut up. He had a motive. Mom says suspects have to have a motive."

"And his motive is?"

"Love. He mopey-dopey loves her. And she doesn't love him back."

"So, like, she won't go out with him so he kidnaps her?"

I have to think about this for a second, but yes. That's pretty much it. "He just flipped out. One day, he loved her so much he couldn't take it anymore, and he went to her house and told her he wanted to marry her and she said, 'Get out,' and he went bonkers and kidnapped her to be his very own."

"Like a caveman?"

"Uh huh. Like a caveman-lobsterman."

"I don't know, Q. It's possible, I guess."

"Well, you don't think she ran away to save the whales, do you?" I cross my arms and dare him to disagree, which I know he won't because he never agrees with his uncle.

"Yeah, my uncle told me that too."

So I continue with my argument. "She was kidnapped, and the kidnapper came back and got some things for her—"

"And cleaned the house?" He shakes his head. "I don't think so."

"He didn't clean the house so it would be clean, you genius. He cleaned so it would look like she went on a trip. But what he doesn't know is that I saw the house after he took her but before he came back and cleaned it up."

"Or maybe he does. Maybe he was lurking in the woods watching you and waiting until you left. *Oooooooooooo.*" He makes spooky fingers, which I slap down.

"Stop it. Be serious."

"If it was Owen Loney," Ben says, "he knows perfectly well you were there, because he was in the café talking to your dad when you ran home. You said so. Don't you think your dad told him where you went?" He crosses his arms back at me. "Like I said, Quinnie, Maiden Rock has no secrets."

"Well, now it does. Someone named Owen Loney has a big secret. He has everything a sheriff needs to arrest him: motive, opportunity, and means—his boat. I bet he took Ms. Stillford on his boat to an island—a place like Oar Island or Spectacle Island or Spruce Island—but you know, even smaller, more private. He's probably hiding her in a fishing cabin."

Ben bounces his foot against the table—*thunk, thunk, thunk.*

"Don't do that. It's annoying," I say. But I can tell he's thinking hard about what I said.

He looks up like something is dawning on him. "There's someone else who has motive, opportunity, and means."

"Who?"

Ben tips his head like I should know who he is talking about. I don't.

"My Uncle John, that's who."

"What?"

"Okay," Ben says. "First, well, I guess it's pretty obvious—she left him at the church, and he still loves her—"

"They broke up."

"They way more than broke up. You don't like to think she'd do it, but she totally didn't show up at the wedding."

He is technically correct. Twenty-five years ago, everyone in Maiden Rock was in the church, and the lobster rolls and macaroni salad and cake were all set up in the basement dining hall, and people had to eat them even though there wasn't a wedding so that the food wouldn't go to waste. Dad said they sent the band home, though.

"I think she was being brave to not marry some-one she didn't love."

"Whatever. He's my uncle, and I can tell you, he's still steamed."

I pick up the milk carton and look in it. Drained. "Fine. Do you want juice?"

Ben rubs his stomach like he's trying to decide. "Nah. But listen, he's always saying little mean things about her when she's not around."

"Okay. Let's say he has a motive."

Ben gets up and starts to pace around the kitchen like he's in court. "You know, he was late meeting me at school on Thursday, and when he did show up, his pickup was totally empty. Like, there was nothing in it. The usual seed, fertilizer, wire, tools—none of that." He spins to face me and slams his hand on the table. "*And* the shell topper was on the pickup."

"Okay," I say. "That's weird."

"When I asked him about it, he said he cleaned the pickup and took it over to Downeast Truck to see what it was worth in trade. And it's only two years old. He *never* trades in a truck that soon."

I scrounge in the kitchen drawer for a pen and paper, without success.

"*And* last night he kept asking me if I'd heard anything about Blythe and if I'd talked to you. *And*, oh, he went out about eight o'clock last night for almost two hours. I waited up for him, and when he got in he was real cranky and told me to 'Get to bed and stop asking questions,' and when I asked him where he went, he said, 'I'm not accountable to you, boy.' I smelled beer on his breath too."

I can't find a darn pen but I'm becoming convinced Ben's right. "Motive, means and opportunity." I sink into a chair and put my face in my hands. The pictures forming in my brain are horrible. Ms. Stillford in the back of John Denby's pickup with her hands and feet tied and maybe a bag over her head. John Denby carrying her over his shoulder like a sack of potatoes from the pickup to—where? My mouth juices up like I might need to barf.

Ben is getting more and more wound up. "I thought maybe the state was talking about shutting down the nature center again and Uncle John was getting fired as director, because that's usually what makes him go out for a beer. And then this morning, he left the house at 5:30 a.m., saying he was going to Gusty's, and took *the Subaru*. Not the truck." I look up, and he's pointing at me. "And he's the kind of guy who'd be quiet for years, then just go bonkers. Am I right? My uncle is a really strange guy."

"And you're not saying this because he's crabby with you all the time?"

"My cross-country coach, Mr. Bisbee, is crabby all the time too, and I'm not saying it's him."

"Means, motive, and opportunity." We repeat it at the same time.

"Just so you know," Ben says, "they say that on *CSI* too. Your mom didn't invent it."

Now I'm thinking hard about Ben's uncle. "He did say that thing about her being in the Save the Whales protest, about her being *flighty*."

"I know. He's trying to make everyone think she went away on her own. Especially your mom."

"Do you think maybe your uncle John and Owen Loney kidnapped her together?"

He laughs. "No way. Those guys hate each other." He stands up and groans. "I have to move. I feel like I have a watermelon in my gut. I think it was the cinnamon bun."

"Or the jar of pickles and the quart of milk."

So for the next two hours we stalk up and down the beach, arguing out scenarios, and getting soaked with sea spray. But we don't come any closer to deciding if it's Owen Loney or Ben's uncle John, or where Ms. Stillford's being hidden.

Then my eye caches sight of a boat speeding out of the channel, slamming into waves as it cuts past the convent.

"Look!" Ben points. "There goes Loney."

"He's heading out to sea—fast." I look at my

phone. It says 1:07 p.m. "Where's he going at this time of day?"

"My uncle said his engine was broken. I guess it got fixed."

"My dad said Owen Loney needed an odd part that would have to be ordered. Besides, here in Maiden Rock, nothing ever gets fixed that fast." I flash back to a whole week last summer when Gusty's old shake mixer died and we had no chocolate malts—even with Mom on the case. "If his engine was ever really broken."

We watch as Owen Loney's boat gets smaller on the horizon. "There are over four thousand islands off the coast of Maine," Ben says.

"Yeah, but we're only looking for one of them," I yell over my shoulder as I run up the beach toward home. "Let's grab a map."

10

Ben studies a map of Maiden Rock and its coastline that my parents framed and hung in our dining room, while I'm in the kitchen trying to bring up Google Maps on my phone.

"There are mermaids on this map," Ben calls out like this is a surprise.

"It's from eighteen hundred something." I stretch the screen with my fingertips. "There are over *four thousand six hundred* islands off the coast of Maine."

"They're waving at the fishermen. And what are these squiggle things?"

"They're serpents. In those days, sailors were either lured onto the rocks by mermaids or eaten by big water snakes." I walk into the dining room just as Ben is doing an all-over body shiver. "This is useless," I say.

He's still looking at the map. "For sure."

"No, this." I wave my phone. Google doesn't even show the names of most of the islands. "We need a better map of the coast."

We search the hall closet, kitchen drawer, and magazine pile in the living room and end up standing in front of Mom's office door.

"Maybe there's one in there," Ben says but doesn't step into the room.

I'm burning with the urge to search the three desks, but I don't step forward either. "Yeah, maybe. But I think I'll ask Dad."

Ben shrugs. "Maybe we should ask Owen Loney for one."

Ben goes home to the nature center with orders to spy on his uncle John, write down everything John Denby does, and text me with updates. I consider sneaking out to investigate the Lobster Pound while Owen Loney is gone, but Mom is due home any minute, and I have no idea what kind of mood she'll be in, so I think maybe I'll stay in my room.

I get my binoculars out of my desk and scan the ocean for Owen Loney's boat. I imagine Ms. Stillford leaning over the side and signaling with her scarf. But mostly, I just spin my rock on the desktop and trace the letters on the Ouija board on my phone case while I wait for a text from Ben.

At about three o'clock, I hear the door open downstairs and noise in Mom's office. I listen at my door until her footsteps are on the stairs, then I run back to my desk and bury my head in my laptop.

Tap. Tap. It's a light, "I'm sorry" kind of tap, but I don't answer.

The doorknob turns, and Mom says, "Quinnie. Can I come in?"

I keep my head down and don't say anything because I know she's coming in anyway.

"We need to talk about this," she says.

I want to talk to her. I want to spin around and tell her about Owen Loney and John Denby having motive, means, and opportunity to kidnap Ms. Stillford. I want to tell her I paid attention when she talked about that sheriff stuff all these years and now I'm using it. But I don't.

"Okay. I'll start," she says. I can tell she has a prepared speech. "I'll speak first as the sheriff, then as your mother." She clears her throat.

I turn around because I am very interested in what the sheriff has to say.

"Speaking as the sheriff, I reviewed the situation. I considered what you told me you saw at the house yesterday and what I saw myself this morning and what I know about Blythe, and I think . . ."

"Something is wrong, right?"

"No. I think that Blythe may have simply gone off on one of her causes like she did in the old days."

"But, what about—"

"Wait, Quinnie. Hear me out. I know how much you love Blythe. But she's got her little faults like we all have. Blythe . . . well, you see . . . she feels deeply about some things—like when she went on that protest walk on the boardwalk at Atlantic City. She just up and disappeared one day, and we didn't know where she was until Abby Butterman saw her on TV wearing a whale costume and waving a sign."

"If she was wearing a whale costume, how did Mrs. Butterman know it was her?"

"It was hot. She was carrying the head."

This is all news to me.

"All I'm saying, Quinnie, is when she's committed to a cause, she takes it to heart and can get so caught up in it that she does some rash things. She's a wonderful person. Sometimes she's a little flighty, that's all."

"Flighty! You're just saying that because that's what Ben's uncle John said. He's trying to convince you that she ran off. He's trying to put you off his trail."

"*His trail?* What trail?"

I grab the notes where I've listed all my facts.

"Read this, Mom. I think you'll agree that John Denby may have kidnapped Ms. Stillford."

She waves her arms around like a maniac, and my papers flutter to the floor. "Oh my God, Quinnette. What is wrong with you? Now it's John Denby? Why on earth would John Denby want to kidnap Blythe Stillford? Am I losing my mind, or have you lost yours?"

I scramble to pick up my papers. "Mom, please. Please, Mom. Look at this."

"No. No. No. No. Who's next? Your father? Me? Who hasn't kidnapped Blythe Stillford?"

I am so overwhelmed by this time that I don't know what to do or say. All that comes out is a weak, "I don't think you or Dad did it."

"Well, thanks for that, Quinn. That's a relief."

I try again. "It was for love!"

"What?"

I spit it out as fast as I can. "Ben's uncle has a motive. He still loves her even though she walked out on the wedding. He has means: his Subaru and his pickup—that he just cleaned squeaky-clean. He has opportunity: he can go anywhere any time he wants because he works alone at the nature center." And then I list the facts for Owen Loney.

Mom chews the inside of her cheek while she waits for me to finish.

"You're accusing two well-respected men in our town of kidnapping. You say one of them abducted Blythe Stillford because he loves her. You say he took her forcibly from her home then went back and gathered her clothes and drugs and cleaned the kitchen. You say this man is hiding her on an island."

"Uh huh." Yes. She gets it!

"Can you tell me what this man hopes to accomplish?"

I try to think of the perfect sheriff's answer. The one that will convince her. "To make her love him. That's what."

Mom's face softens. I'm not sure if it means she believes me or she's sad. I hope it means she's going to tell me I'm right and help me find Ms. Stillford.

"How old are you now, Quinn?" It's one of those questions she already knows the answer to. "You are thirteen, Quinn, and I am sorry to say, you don't *really* know all there is to know about Blythe Stillford *or* Owen Loney *or* John Denby. And, honey, you don't really know love. No matter how much you love someone, you can't force them to love you back. By kidnapping or any other way."

"What if you're a maniac psycho-killer lover?"

Then Mom does the worst thing she could do.

She laughs. "Quinnie, I'm no criminal-profiling psychiatrist, but I've had plenty of crime investigation training. I've known these two men my whole life, and I don't think either one of them is a maniac psycho-killer lover."

I grab my hair like I want to pull it out. "Erhhhh!"

"Q—stop. I'm not saying there aren't such people, but those types are generally loners. They have personal histories that are very specific. Owen and John don't fit the profile. And I can't see how love is a motive. It makes more sense that Blythe took off and forgot about school."

"She wouldn't forget about me, Mom."

"Oh, honey."

It hits me at that moment: I can't count on Mom the Sheriff, Mom the Mayor, Mom the Real Estate Lady, or Mom the Postmaster to help me find Ms. Stillford. I am alone. Okay, not alone-alone. I have to do it myself—with Ben. Mom is wrong that Ms. Stillford is safe, and she is wrong about love. I do know about love. I know that if you love someone true enough and long enough and hard enough, they will love you back, even if they are treating you like a cousin right now.

"And Quinn," Mom says with a sharper tone, "I don't want any more accusations. I don't want any sneaking around investigating anyone or anything. I don't want any more interfering with Blythe's life. Do you understand?"

"But—"

"No buts. No nothing. Do you understand?"

There is only one answer to this question that will set me free to search for Ms. Stillford. A simple, un-arguing *yes*, and she will leave, and I can get on with it.

"Yes."

* * *

When Dad gets home, I stand at the top of the stairs and catch bits and pieces of Mom telling him all about my "overdramatizing."

"Now, don't *you* go overreacting," Dad says.

"I do not overreact, Gus."

"It's odd . . . first day of school . . ."

". . . wish to heck Blythe would just call me . . . let me know where she is."

At about six o'clock, I hear floorboards groan and plates clink. On the other side of my door is a message in the form of a crab cake sandwich. I can't remember if I've eaten all day. It tastes good. I check my phone. No texts from Ben.

As I lay in bed at night, my brain keeps flipping between Owen Loney and John Denby, and I try to imagine one of them taking Ms. Stillford out of her house—and then what? She screams, right? Does the kidnapper drug her? Does he knock her on the head? Does she go willingly? Does he trick her? I know he surprises her because of the apple and the uncapped peanut butter jar.

By nine o'clock, the convent lights have snapped on. They throw harsh light down the beach all the way to our house. The sisters started this last spring, and the renters grumbled about it all summer. Mom couldn't get them to stop.

All Sister Rosie said was, "I know dear, but we're all alone here, and it makes us feel safer." Sister Ethel added, "It's just a little comfort, dear."

"I understand, sisters," Mom snapped, "but most people are comforted with something a little less Times Square–like."

And when Mom complained about it at Gusty's, Ms. Stillford said, "Phoo, Margaret, let them be."

I listen to the surf through the closed window, crashing in and pulling out. Dad says it's like counting sheep for Maiden Rockers. But whether it's going *shssssh*, like Ms. Stillford says, or going *baaaa*, like Dad says, I can't sleep.

II

I wake up Sunday morning and immediately check my phone. No calls and no texts.

I call Ms. Stillford's number. My call goes immediately to voice mail. I think something horrific—the phone is at the bottom of the ocean. I call Ben and ask him, "Do you have anything to report?"

"Nah. He's reading the paper and drinking coffee."

"Watch him and text me," I remind him, but I can tell he's not focused on spying at the moment. He's absorbed in Ace Hood and Nicki. It only makes one of my ears bleed a little. I know for him it isn't the words. He can't even tell you the words. It's the pounding in his blood when he listens to it. It matches the pounding of his feet. That boy can run to the beat forever. But dance? Nope.

"Call me, text me!" I say again.

"Okay. Okay. But I gotta get out of here for a while. Go for a run."

I hear something like worry in his voice, like he's thinking being in the house with his uncle isn't such a good idea.

"I think you're safe. He's only in criminal love with Ms. Stillford," I offer.

There's a silence, then Ben laughs a little. "Yeah, well, he doesn't even love me as much as that new nest of bobolinks, so I guess I'm safe."

The last thing I say to him before I hang up is, "Run fast."

* * *

By noon, I'm itching to walk up to Loney's Lobster Pound and look around, but Mom is sitting at her real estate desk like a prison guard. I could say I want to go for a walk on the beach. How could she deprive me of that? My beach, my seaweed, my gulls, nature, science, marine biology, ecology—it's almost like school. That's it. I'll tell her I'm taking a science walk to make up for the missed first day of school.

When Mom says "No way," I'm back in my room, writing Zoe a letter. She doesn't have any Internet on the Scottish sheep farm.

Z –

By the time you get this, hopefully Ms. Stillford will be safe. She didn't show for the first day of school, and I think it's because she's been kidnapped by either Owen Loney or your uncle John. Mom refuses to believe me. She thinks Ms. Stillford is saving the whales. Wish you were here. Boo hoo. Write me! This is so scary. Don't tell anyone I told you this because I am not supposed to be butting into Ms. Stillford's life—even though someone should be—meaning THE SHERIFF!

XOXOXOXOXO

Q

I take out my binoculars and watch for Owen Loney's lobster boat. Nothing. I try to remember what else was taken from Ms. Stillford's house. My mind is blank. I spin my rock. My cell phone is face down on my desk. I stare out the window.

The Ouija board case vibrates. Ben's reports start rolling in: *He's eating potato chips.*

Me: *Not very incriminating.*

Ben: *He wants to know if I want wild rice soup for dinner.*

Me: *OMG! Ms. S hearts WRS!*

Ben: *So does all of Maine*

Me: *What did you tell him?*

Ben: *No. I pigged out on 3 PBJs after my run.*

Me: *What's he doing now?*

Ben: *Making WRS anyway.*

Me: *See! He must be making it for her.*

Ben: *He's putting it in a plastic container in the fridge.*

Me: *Did he eat any of it?*

Ben: *Don't think so.*

12

My dreams are filled with pictures of Ms. Stillford gagged and tied to a chair. She shakes her head like she's refusing something.

I wake up late Monday morning with a nasty stomachache, reach for my rock, and snuggle under my comforter. The clock tells me Dad is long gone, but I hear mumbling down in Mom's office.

The sound of her voice irritates me. If she'd only listened to me, we might have already rescued Ms. Stillford from some remote fishing cabin. Life would be back to normal, if life can ever go back to normal after you're kidnapped and tied up in a dank cabin with . . . cold wild rice soup? I imagine what it would feel like to be shivering and tied to a chair with someone you hate sticking a spoonful of soup in your face. It probably dribbles on your shirt.

Ack! I throw off the covers and jump out of bed

to shake the idea out of my head. I don't get dressed or anything. I just storm right down to Mom's office, where she's just hanging up the phone. She looks tired but not mad.

"It's Monday morning, Mom."

"I know."

"And she's not here."

"I know."

"And that's not right."

"I know. I know. It may not be."

"So, you'll do something?"

* * *

Mom's idea of doing something is to call the morgue, and when Ms. Stillford isn't there, to call hospitals. Listening to her give a physical description of Ms. Stillford over the phone shakes me. It makes the disappearance more real. At 10:00, I hear the US Post Office regional truck wind its way into town, grind its brakes, and turn up Mile Stretch Road. I know Mom is watching it from her office window.

"I'm going to do the mail," she calls up the stairs. "Do you want anything from Gusty's for lunch? Maybe you should do some reading in your schoolbooks. This is the second day of school. Do some reading, at least."

"Mom! This is a crisis!"

"All right. All right."

"Fried egg sandwich," I call out.

It doesn't take long to deliver the mail in Maiden Rock. The summer people rarely get mail, and after Labor Day, there's almost nobody around. But it usually takes longer than ten minutes, which is when Mom comes speeding back and pounds up the steps into the house.

"Quinnie! I got a letter from Blythe!"

I run downstairs. She's in the kitchen, working her hands into surgical gloves.

"Why are you putting those on?"

"Normal procedure," Mom says.

"Normal procedure for what? I thought you said she was saving whales. Why do you need procedure for whale saving?"

She ignores me and uses tweezers to take the letter out of the envelope. A single sheet falls to the table. It's creased in two places like the start of an origami design.

I reach for it.

"Wait. Don't touch it," Mom orders. She buzzes around the table, taking pictures of the letter with her phone.

"Have you read it?"

"Not yet."

Her sudden shift into concerned sheriff mode frightens me. "Is it a ransom note?"

"I don't know yet."

She flips the envelope over and takes a picture of the postmark. I lean over and read it. *HOULTON. MAINE. September 13, 2015.*

"Where's Houlton?" I ask.

"Up 95, near the border, just before you get to Ontario." She takes a clear plastic bag from the drawer and slides the letter into it, then presses it flat with her hands and pushes it toward me. "Let's read it. Take your time."

I sit down at the table next to Mom. With our heads almost touching, we read in silence. In my head, Ms. Stillford is speaking.

13

Dear Margaret,

Forgive me for rushing off the way I did. I wish I could have given some advanced notice, but my cousin showed up and told me that our great auntie is failing. We are gathering at her bedside in Ontario. She is a 93-year-old nun and has been very special to so many of us cousins.

I tossed some things in my cousin's car and off we went. I forgot my cell phone but that's no loss since the reception there is nil. I have no idea when I'll be home.

Would you also tell Owen Loney he can go ahead and repair my broken window frame on the top floor facing the convent?

I'm dropping this in the mailbox in Houlton. I hope it arrives by Friday. My apologies to Quinnie for not calling to cancel Friday morning. Please ask

*her to put my mail on my desk. And please pray for
a quick and peaceful resolution.*

Blythe

*Wait, sorry. Forgot to mail this. And I should
tell you that another cousin who is coming up from
Boston will be stopping by the house to get my
phone and a few things, so don't be concerned if
it looks like someone was there. Now, I will send
this with another cousin who is going to Houlton
for groceries. He promises he will get it in the mail
Saturday afternoon.*

*I know it sounds like there are a lot of cousins.
There are.*

All the best,

Blythe

I look at Mom. She's waiting expectantly for my
response.

"It's wrong," I say.

"Is it her handwriting?" Mom asks. "You see it
more than anybody."

She isn't kidding around. She totally wants to
know what I think. I look again, closer.

It has her familiar bold *D* on the "Dear," with
its slanty swoop. And there's her curly *ing.* It makes

me happy. I want to trace my finger over it. The words are evenly spaced like tiles on a scrabble board. I always wondered how she managed that. "Yes. I think it is. No, I know it is. But it's like somebody was telling her, 'Write it or else.'"

"Focus, Quinnie. Just tell me exactly what you think is wrong about it."

I shake my head as if to clear my mind and look at the letter again. Sentence by sentence. As far as I'm concerned, it's filled with clues that cry out, "I am not okay. Help me."

"Well, first of all, I never, ever heard of this ninety-three-year-old nun that has been *very special* to her. She told me about her grandmother, Tootsie, who was an aircraft mechanic during World War II. She told me about her two twin-boy cousins in Bangor who knocked out each other's front teeth wrestling around the living room and who are both dentists now. She showed me the photo of her family reunion in Ontario and pointed to every face and told me every name and every funny story. And there was *no old nun*."

"Go on."

"Well, the part about telling Owen Loney to fix her window. She already told him that. I was standing right there in Gusty's, next to both of them, when she told him to go ahead. And she knows I heard that, which could mean she's trying to mention his name so we know he kidnapped her."

"Wait, don't go there. Try not to read the letter to prove what you think. Just tell me what's suspicious about it."

She isn't mad when she says it. It's like she's decided to let me help, like a real detective.

"The whole part about another cousin coming from Boston to explain the missing stuff, especially the part where the kitchen gets cleaned up, it's too much trying to explain. And if the cousin got her cell phone, why didn't she call us?"

"It could be dead and without a charger," Mom says. "But what else?"

"At least she's not dead. She wrote this letter."

Mom doesn't say anything. She looks out the kitchen door to the ocean.

"Mom?"

She turns to me and touches my hand. "I'm sorry."

I don't know everything she's sorry about but I get it that she's sorry she didn't take me seriously about Ms. Stillford. And my chest swells up with love for her and her simple, straight-from-the-heart apology.

"Your instincts were right," Mom says. "It's so complicated, Quinnie."

Wait. Now it's complicated. I sense a big *but* coming. There is always a big *but* coming when she says it's complicated. It's usually followed by *you wouldn't understand.*

"I should have been more open to your concerns, but Blythe does have a history, and you just can't go around wildly accusing people of such things." She's talking more to herself than to me.

"But"—now I'm the one saying *but*—"you agree something's wrong?"

"I do. Now go get those pages of notes you tried to show me the other day."

14

One thing about my mom the sheriff. Once she gets on the scent of a crime, she is a bloodhound. Actually, my mom the real-estate lady follows the scent of a sale the same way, and Mom the mayor? Well, she's been reelected seven times. Another thing about her? She's stubborn. So, I guess it's no surprise that we can't agree on what to do next.

We're in her office. I'm sitting in the guest chair. She's in the sheriff's chair. She compliments my notes, says I've done a great job and that I was right to concentrate on motive, means, and opportunity. Together, we make a list of suspects.

"It's statistically likely to be someone she knows," Mom says.

At number one, I put *Owen Loney* and at number two, *John Denby*. At number three, Mom writes, *Someone from out of town but who knows Blythe Stillford,* and at number four, *Someone from out of town who doesn't know Blythe Stillford.*

Then we talk about our suspects' opportunities to kidnap her, go back into her house, and mail a letter in Houlton no later than 3:00 p.m. on Saturday the thirteenth. A postmaster knows pick-up times.

We don't know when she was kidnapped exactly, but I attempt to persuade Mom that Owen Loney *could have* gone to her house at dinnertime on Thursday to fix the screen and *could have* used his boat to take her somewhere. He was in Gusty's Friday morning and he *could have* gone to her house after I was there. He *could have* driven up to Houlton and back on Saturday *except* for the fact that Ben and I saw him going out to sea early Saturday afternoon. Okay, he's not an absolutely perfect suspect.

I also argue that John Denby *could have* gone to Ms. Stillford's house at dinnertime on Thursday. It is strange that he cleaned his pickup on Friday. Maybe there was blood in it. He was in Gusty's Friday afternoon, but we don't know where he was Friday morning. *Except*, it would have been hard for him to be in Houlton, since it takes eight hours round trip. Ben would have missed him on Saturday if he'd been away that long. Okay, he's not an absolutely perfect suspect either.

So Mom argues that her two suspect ideas should move to the top of the list.

"Owen Loney and John Denby both have the motive—love. Stop shaking your head, Mom!"

Mom shakes her head harder. "That's just not reasonable, plausible, or credible. I don't buy it."

"So who has the motive, then?" I demand.

"Someone who thinks Blythe has something that's worth money. Jewelry, maybe."

"So why wouldn't they just take it?"

"It could have been a burglary that went wrong. Maybe she surprises them, puts up a fight, and they decide to take her along to keep her quiet." Mom sounds like she's convincing herself. "And they come back for the medicine and the clothes. Which suggests they know her and care about her—or at least that they're not killers."

"So where is she? Where did they take her?"

Mom digs through a pile of papers on her desk and comes up with her iPad. "Suppose," she says as she taps Google Maps and zeros in on northern Maine, "it's a young, strong man who is either in the family or knows the family. He hears she has something valuable and comes to steal it. He finds her home and he panics. He doesn't want to be discovered, so he grabs her and drives north. He knows he can't take her across the border, so he takes her somewhere deep in the woods. He gets her to write the letter, and he mails it in Houlton. She figures it's safer to play along."

She looks at me like she expects me to agree. I have to admit I can see it. I can picture it.

I tip the iPad so I can reach the screen, and I swipe it toward the coast. Maybe this bigger screen will have a better display of the islands. "Let's say it's Owen Loney—"

"Quinnie, if you're going to do this right, you can't have a one-track mind."

"My one-track mind, *Mom*, is that I want to find Ms. Stillford. Now, listen, Owen Loney takes her to a remote island on his fishing boat. Or John Denby hides her in the woods in a cabin. And she thinks if she's nice to him, he'll eventually come to his senses and let her go."

Mom stands up and paces while she listens and then says, "If Owen Loney kidnapped her, he'd never let her put his name in the letter."

"Okay, then what about John Denby? He wouldn't care if she named Owen Loney in the letter. It would take suspicion off of him."

"Nope. If John Denby lets her put Owen Loney in the letter, he's eliminating Loney as a suspect. It's the opposite of what you said."

All of a sudden I remember something and run upstairs, yelling, "Wait, Mom, wait!"

I rip through my room and find my backpack under a pile of clothes. I root around in it until find what I'm looking for, then rush back down to the kitchen.

"This is Blythe's lobster pin," Mom says as I uncurl my fingers. "Where did you get it?"

"It was on the floor at the café. I found it Friday morning. I saw it on her scarf on Thursday. It must have fallen off. It was on the floor by our table."

"Or the thief took it from her house and later dropped it at Gusty's," Mom says.

I get goosebumps. "The kidnapper may have been in Gusty's, and we didn't even know it."

"For all we know, Blythe may have been tied up in the trunk in the parking lot while he ate a lobster roll," Mom says. She sees my lip tremble and hugs me.

"I'm sorry I said that," she whispers. "I shouldn't involve you any deeper in this."

A shiver goes up my spine and I remember how I was standing next to the Escalade and I had an inkling that Ms. Stillford was in the back. I'm about to tell Mom about it, but she holds my shoulders straight and looks into my eyes and says, "All right, here's what we're going to do."

15

Mom gets on the phone and files a missing persons report. I offer her my version, but she pulls up a form online and shows me how all you have to do is fill in the blanks. Then she calls the Houlton police, the border patrol, and the FBI. At three that afternoon, the field investigation begins, with headquarters at Gusty's. Police and volunteers from nearby towns crowd in, and each person picks a dark blue jacket from a big cardboard box. The jackets shout *RESCUE* in neon yellow letters across the back.

Dad flips burger after burger to feed the hungry searchers and keeps trying to push one on me.

"Dad! For the third time, I do *not* want a burger." A burger would taste like sand right now. "Ben wants a burger. Give him one."

Ben and I sit at our table in the corner. John

Denby is nowhere to be seen. I show him a copy of the missing persons report:

Blythe Stillford was reported missing on Monday, September 15. Stillford lives in Maiden Rock, Maine, and is a retired high school chemistry teacher currently working as a tutor. She was last seen on Thursday, September 11, at Gusty's Café. The circumstances of her disappearance are considered suspicious.

At the time of her disappearance she was 60 years of age, stood 5' 4", and weighed approximately 130 pounds. When last seen she was wearing blue jeans, a green sweater, a silk scarf, boat shoes, and cat-eye glasses. She carried a canvas tote that says "Beatrix Potter's Botanicals."

Anyone knowing anything about the whereabouts of Blythe Stillford, please contact the Maiden Rock sheriff, Margaret Boyd, at #10 Mile Stretch Road, Maiden Rock, Maine, or online at www.maidenrocksheriff.gov.

I don't like seeing her age, height, and weight "at the time of her disappearance," because it makes her sound like a body instead of a live person, but Mom says that's how it's done.

"Look up here, folks," Mom calls out. "Here's a picture of Blythe Stillford."

She holds it up so everyone can see it. The photo comes from our last Fourth of July picnic. Ms. Stillford's wearing her traditional red-and-white striped sailor top and bell-bottom jeans. The ones she calls *vintage*. Two women in the group whisper and smile. I think they're making fun of Ms. Stillford's clothes. I want to run over and yell at them to get out.

"She's sixty years old, approximately one hundred and thirty pounds, has long blonde hair with silver streaks. She usually wears it in a loose knot at her neck. When she was last seen, she had on a green sweater, a silk scarf, jeans, and boat shoes. Oh, and glasses. She wears brown cat-eye frames with orange stones at the corners."

"Last seen when?" a big guy with a gold badge asks. He looks at the others like Mom is screwing up the investigation by talking about the orange stones.

"I'm getting to that, Officer Dobson." Mom gives him a stare. "She was last seen here in Gusty's. She had lunch with my daughter, Quinnette, last Thursday." She turns to me. "Quinnie, come tell us what happened at lunch."

I shrink in my chair. I'd been so eager to get this going. Now, in front of all these people I don't want the spotlight anywhere near me. Mom walks over and pulls me up by my elbow.

"Go ahead, honey. Tell them what happened."

I search the room for my dad and find him behind the counter. He gives me a you-can-do-it nod. Mom's thumb is pressing a little too hard into my arm. I know it's because she needs me to do my part.

"She had a Gusty Burger . . ." I falter a bit. *Just the facts, right?*

The big guy smirks, which gets a couple other people looking down and stifling laughs. Now I hate him for sure. Mom slips her arm around my shoulder and squeezes.

"She had on her lobster pin, and she was pretty normal, kind of." I stand up a little straighter. "I showed her my new school clothes and my notebooks and my Ouija Board phone case." Okay, I'm starting to babble.

When I start to show the crowd my phone case, Mom says, "Anything else, Quinnie?" She can tell my mind is drifting to the brown apple and the lobster pin on the floor, and she jumps in. "About the last time you saw her. That's what we need to hear right now."

I know so much, but Mom told me not to tell anyone about her letter or what I saw in her house. "Owen Loney was there. He was talking to her about fixing a torn screen at her house."

The room falls quiet. I look around and accidentally make eye contact with Officer Dobson.

"Who's Owen Loney?" Officer Dobson reaches into his shirt pocket and takes out a small spiral pad and ballpoint pen. One of his big thumbs flips to a blank page; the other clicks the pen tip up and down.

"I'm Owen Loney," a gruff voice calls from the back of the crowd.

All heads turn toward the door, to the man wearing the *Lobstah!* cap. Ben and I stretch our necks to see him.

"Come on up here where people can see you, Owen," Mom says, and she shoots me a look. "And tell us what you remember about Thursday afternoon."

Owen Loney shoulders his way through the blue-jacketed volunteers. He stands with his gnarly knuckled hands clasped in front of him. His brow wrinkles with worry lines.

"I had my regular number three, crab cake sandwich with fries, and was finishing up my second cup of coffee when Blythe came in, so I went over and talked to her about it getting windier and all, and did she want me to fix up her torn screen on the second floor on the ocean side."

He swallows and waits.

Mom prompts him to continue. "What did she say, Owen?"

"She said, 'Sure, thanks.'"

A little titter of laughter goes through the crowd, like that was a silly answer.

"Were those her exact words?" asks Dobson.

"Let me see." Owen rubs his whiskery chin and studies the floor for a couple seconds. "I believe she said, 'Thanks, Owen. I'd like that.' But I don't know what good knowing that is. We ought to be out looking for her right now."

Murmurs ripple through the crowd. Owen Loney adjusts his cap, pulling it down tight.

"Did you see her leave?" someone calls from the back.

"Nope. I left before she did."

"Did you see anyone else? Anyone drive by?" Dobson asks.

"Not a soul . . . 'cept the sisters."

"What sisters?"

"The nuns. Them two that live at the convent out on the point and drive like it's the Indy 500."

A few little conversations break out.

"Yes, well, now let's break up into groups," Mom says to the crowd. "I'll come around and give you each a map and a search area. And you don't have to deal with the beach houses. I've got keys for all of them, and I'll be checking each one later this afternoon."

16

In between people calling out "Over here" and
"I'll go with Joe" and "Put me on the yacht club
group," the café door opens and a man and a girl
make their way through the crowd. The man is tall
with a pale, rectangular face and small eyes framed
by chunky tortoiseshell glasses. The girl is thin, with
long, dark hair; red lips; and skinny jeans marked by
thready holes.

I immediately know who they are and who they
might be looking for—Real Estate Mom. I try to
catch Mom's eye, but she's sucked into the confusion
of search teams sorting themselves out.

I go to the kitchen. Dad is inching four molten-
hot blueberry pies out of the oven.

"The Zoe house people are here," I say. I know
if I say the Philpotts are here, he'll say "Who?" He
doesn't remember rental-people names. That space in

his brain is reserved for things like the unusual garlic salad dressing on the coleslaw at Betty's Tea Room in Boston that closed before I was born.

His face slowly shows recognition.

"Oh, boy. Where's your Mom? She needs this right now like a gull needs a bath. And I can't leave the café." I don't remind him that gulls are filthy things that could all use a good scrubbing. I already researched that at Ms. Stillford's request.

I peek out front. Most searchers have cleared out of the café, and the Philpotts man is standing in the middle of the room with his hands on his hips like the Jolly Green Giant. The girl slouches by a table, chewing on the end of her hoodie string. Cars are pulling out of the parking lot, and search teams are scattering in every direction. Mom is nowhere to be seen.

I turn back to the kitchen. Dad sticks four other pies, unbaked, into the oven.

"Go home and get the keys for the Buttermans' out of Mom's office. Okay, honey? And let them in."

"They saw all the police. I think they might be changing their minds," I say. "I'll see if they still—"

"*Quinnie*," Dad says. "Don't start."

There are a few reasons why I don't want to show these people to #9 Mile Stretch Road. First of all, it is Zoe's personal house. Second, I don't need a replacement friend for Zoe, despite what Mom says. And, oh, third, and most important, they will just be in the way of the investigation to find Ms. Stillford. And fourth, I don't want to go to school with their daughter. I want it to be like Ms. Stillford said: "It's you and me, kid." So I don't go get the keys right away. Instead, I walk up to the man and the girl.

"Are you the Philpotts?" I ask.

The man turns to me. "What's going on here?"

"There's a missing person," I say.

"*Really.* Who's missing?" He acts interested in a detached way, like he might make it a scene in one of his books someday, which gets me, because I do not want him writing about Ms. Stillford. This isn't some mystery novel. This is real life.

"Blythe Stillford."

The man looks at the girl. "Isn't she the tutor?"

I think of Ms. Stillford showing me an article about a big oil spill in the Gulf of Mexico with a picture of a red-faced man ranting and raving about his vacation getting ruined because he couldn't go on the beach. "What's sad about this story, Quinnie, is that too often a problem is only as big to people as the part of it that affects them."

It's true. Ms. Stillford's kidnapping is just a school problem for the Philpotts. I look at the girl, and her face is zoned like she didn't hear it or like she has practice tuning it out.

Mr. Philpotts pats his pockets until he locates his phone and a slip of paper. I guess I'm not important enough to talk to.

The girl continues to lean against a table. I notice for the first time she has glittery green on her eyelids and her eyes are icy blue. I look at Ben. He's stealing glances at the girl from behind *World Cultures: Western Hemisphere.*

The man clears his throat and puts the paper in his pocket. He has just pulled out one of those electronic cigarettes when I hear a ten-second loop of "Glory Days" and turn to see my mom's cell phone lighting up on the counter. Springsteen continues to play a few bars.

Mr. Philpotts turns his back to me and tucks his chin. The girl looks at the phone on the counter, then at her dad, who puts his finger in his free ear to block out the Boss. I notice his daughter isn't actually wearing lipstick. Her lips are stained scarlet like she had it on yesterday.

Mom's phone stops ringing, and the man stands up tall. "Hello, this is Jack Philpotts. Leaving a message for Margaret Boyd. We're here in Maiden Rock. At the café . . . at"—he looks around, then grabs a menu—"Gusty's." He tosses the menu back on the table. "I guess we've arrived in the middle of a crisis, but we'd like to get into our house. Please call me as soon as possible." He presses *END* and turns to the girl and says, "We might as well sit down. It could be a while."

The girl doesn't move.

"Do you want anything?" I ask them. "Coffee? Pie?"

"You work here?" the girl asks me.

"My dad's Gusty."

The girl twirls her hoodie strings a few more revolutions and looks over at Ben like she'd like to know who he is. I don't volunteer anything.

"Coffee, maybe . . . sure, two coffees," Mr. Philpotts says. He looks at the girl but she doesn't move. "Come on, kiddo. Might as well have a seat." She sits down, and he drops his head and starts tapping on his phone again.

With my left hand, I hook two mugs, and with my right hand, I grab the pot of Columbian decaf.

The man looks up, "Is that leaded?"

It takes me a second.

"Decaf," I say. "That's all Gusty brews after noon."

"I guess that will have to do, then." He resumes his phone absorption.

I don't reply. Dad says when customers say rude things, just count one—one thousand, two—one thousand in your head and then move on.

The café door flies open as Mom rushes in and scans the room. The second she spies her phone on the counter, "Glory Days" launches again.

"Oh my God, there it is." Mom runs to catch the call. "Hello, yes."

She heads toward the kitchen, still talking on the phone. Her voice grates, "Yes, Officer Dobson . . . I *know* that, I live here . . ."

The café door swings open again, interrupting my eavesdropping, and John Denby walks in.

"Quinnie." He nods at me like my name itself is hello enough. The hair on the back of my neck stands up. He looks at Ben and says, "Have you done your homework?"

Ben flips open a notebook and starts writing.

"My mom's in the back," I say and look behind the counter.

John Denby slides onto a counter stool.

"Coffee?" I ask him.

"No, thanks."

I want to ask him where he's been all morning to

see if he'll slip and say, "Taking care of my darling," but I know he won't. So I don't. I know he normally spends his mornings filling bird feeders and tromping around in Becker's Woods. That what naturalists do, I guess.

"You going on a search team?" John Denby asks me while he folds a paper napkin about five ways— nervous behavior, if you ask me.

I nod and say, "Mom's giving me and Ben our own map."

Over at his table, Mr. Philpotts is still scrolling through emails. The girl is twirling her hair, elbows propped on the table.

"That's good. You two ought to be helping out," John Denby says.

Oh, yeah? Funny how he didn't come in time to join a search team.

He unfolds the napkin again. I want Mom to hurry up and come out and see the nervous behavior.

I go back to my table and to Ben, who is doodling. The girl doesn't look at us but she leans back in her chair now, in our direction, with her hair behind her ear. Listening to us.

Ben's eyes shift back to me. "Who's she?"

I feel a wave of . . . I don't know exactly what . . . jealousy? Here we are getting ready to go on a search that could lead to the discovery of Ms. Stillford, and I am distracted by what Ben thinks of some blue-eyed, red-lipped, skinny jeans-wearing New York girl.

I scoot my chair closer to Ben and whisper, "The people who are renting Zoe's for the winter."

The girl nods slightly, and her hair falls over her ear. It isn't great hair but it's not bad. She's got those sweepy bangs that she swings out of her eyes with a little jerk of her head. I get it why Ben looks. So now I'm getting a stomachache on top of a stomachache.

Mom sticks her head out of the kitchen and looks directly at the Philpotts. She must have listened to her voice mail. Then she notices John Denby. She walks over to him and rests her hand on the counter.

"Thanks for coming, John. I'm thinking your best search area would be the preserve and especially"—she lowers her voice—"the marsh area."

What are you doing, Mom? I scream in my head. *Why would you put a possible killer in charge of the search?*

"Sure. I can do it," John says.

"I'll send someone with you."

"No need. I know that marsh like I know the back of my hand."

See, Mom! He wants to do it alone. Don't let him.

"I know you do," says Mom, "but it's investigation protocol that we have a sweep done by at least three people in a team. So just hang on here for a minute while I get you a couple buddies."

Okay, so Mom is pretty smart. With that simple question, she found out he wanted to search the marsh alone. Ben's shoe touches mine under the table. Then he gives me a knowing look that says: *See, he wants to search the marsh alone.*

Dad slides a plate with a lobster roll and slaw in front of John Denby, who doesn't look in a hurry all of a sudden.

Then, as if a switch flips in Mom's multitasking brain, she puts on her Margaret Boyd Real Estate Lady face and walks over to Mr. Philpotts with her hand extended.

"Mr. Philpotts, how do you do? I'm Margaret Boyd. I spoke to you about the rental."

Mr. Philpotts's eyes shift around the café, trying to make sense of who is who and what is what.

He shakes Mom's hand. "Jack Philpotts," he says like she didn't just say his name to him. Then, like he almost forgot the girl was there, "Oh, and this is my daughter, Mariella."

"Yes, yes. I'm sorry," Mom says. "I left my phone here in the café. I just got your message."

"You're the sheriff?" Jack Philpotts asks, a little confused.

"Yes. I'm the sheriff of Maiden Rock, the mayor of Maiden Rock, and the real estate broker. The postmaster too." She allows it to sink in. "It's a really small town."

"Interesting," says Jack Philpotts again, with a tone that suggests this might be another good thing to put in one of his murder mysteries. "We heard about the teacher situation."

Mom stiffens.

I already don't like the famous author, but I am undecided about this Mariella. What's up with those shoes? I lean enough to look at them again. They're black high-tops on four-inch wedges. I don't even get how she walks in them. I look at Ben, and he's looking at them too.

"Kinky," he says.

"Mmm-hmm," I say, but I'm not sure if he means kinky-good or kinky-weird. I know I mean kinky-weird. This girl is wildly different from Zoe. By now, Zoe would have been at my table, finding out my life history. Maybe Mariella doesn't care. Maybe she's too good for us.

"Let's get you to number nine." Mom switches to her mayor voice. "You'll be right next to us. We're at number ten. Best spot on the beach. Always plowed out first." She motions to me to come over to her, then turns to the Philpotts. "This is my daughter, Quinnie. And this is Ben Denby."

I don't move a muscle. Ben twitches.

Jack Philpotts gives us a little rubber-band smile.

Mariella says, "Hey," and jerks her bangs.

17

Out in the parking lot, Ben says to Mariella, "So. You can hang out with us if you want."

He jiggles his leg like he's got a calf cramp.

"We're not exactly hanging out," I say. I want to pinch him, but I reach into my pocket for my rock. It's not there! What did I do with it? Maybe I left it on my desk. "I mean, we're going to be searching for Ms. Stillford."

Inside Gusty's, Jack Philpotts is listening to Mom and watching her point toward the post office. When she doubles her point like she means Rook River is farther north, he nods.

"I guess. Sure," Mariella says.

So, now I'm stuck with this situation, which I might not mind if Ben wasn't acting so interested in this odd girl. Mom has given us directions to go up and down Mile Stretch Road and scour it for clues. From the convent at number one all the way to the Abbotts' at twenty-eight. How much walking Mariella Philpotts will be able to do in those shoes, I can't guess.

"Okay," I say, taking charge. "Ready? We're headed toward the convent."

No one moves.

"Ready?" I say again.

"Yep," Mariella says.

I can see Ben sizing himself up against her to see if he's taller.

"Ben?" I ask.

"Uh huh." He gives up the height assessment. "Let's go."

"Soooo, we are walking north." I point toward Circle Lane. "Look for personal stuff: Ms. Stillford's scarf, a tote bag that says *Beatrix Potter Botanicals*, a scrap of paper with writing on it—you know, anything that might be a clue to where she is."

Ben adds, "A shoe, a pool of blood, signs of a struggle, a circular burn pattern in the grass from the rocket thrusters of the alien spacecraft." He looks at Mariella like he's checking to see if she thinks he's funny. I want to scream.

Above us, a few gulls cry for the French fries they expect when anyone comes out of Gusty's. When we don't toss fries their way, the gulls screech at us and take off.

"What's your name?" Ben says. "Maryellen?"

"Mariella." The girl stops and stares him straight in the face. "But I prefer Ella. Like Ella Marvell in her *Trouble* period."

"Huh?" says Ben. He squirms out of her stare.

Okay, so she's not shy.

"You don't have a clue what I'm talking about, do you?" she says and keeps walking.

"Don't think so," he says.

Ella Marvell. I search my mental music database. Blues? I'm pretty sure it's not hip-hop or Ben would have nodded some respect.

"Ben likes hip-hop," I volunteer.

"Ella Marvell was the uncontested queen of 1960s rhythm and blues," Mariella says without looking at us.

I kind of doubt that, but I vow to check it out later. I can hear Ms. Stillford saying to her, "Tell me, Mariella. Do you have any support for that statement?" I don't know what Mariella's—or Ella's—schooling has been like up until now, but I bet she'll have to work harder with Ms. Stillford . . . and watch the exaggeration. Or as Ms. Stillford always says to me, "Hew out hyperbole, Quinnie."

I scoop up a handful of sand and broken shells, shift them around in my hand like there might be a clue in the sifting, then pitch them aside and continue on.

Ella walks next to me, if you can call what she does in her crazy-high shoes walking, and Ben follows behind us. I make a metal note to write Zoe about this strange girl from New York.

A few steps later, Ella takes a dive. Not a flat-on-her-face, looking-stupid dive. No. It's more like a fainting swan fall—right back into Ben, whose hands magically catch her under the arms and bounce her back to her feet. Almost like a choreographed move. Ella dips. Ben catches and lifts. She resumes walking. And in that split second, some teeny-weeny little moment happens between them. Some indescribable thing that I know will niggle at me for a long time. Of course, they both pretend not to notice.

We continue walking. Me and them. But their moment nicks away a cubic millimeter of my heart.

Not only that, physical contact with Ella opens up a spigot in Ben. He starts telling her about how we are pretty sure Ms. Stillford's been kidnapped—because of love—by either Owen Loney or his uncle John. And about Ms. Stillford's house and the things being moved and the dresses. He's gushing like Spouting

Rock. He even tells Ella about how his uncle made this big pot of wild rice soup and packed up most of it.

But Ben kind of gets me going too. Soon we're laying out our case, clue by clue. I tell Ella about the timing of Owen Loney taking his boat out the other morning and about John Denby's pickup being all cleaned up with the topper on it. We end on Ms. Stillford's turning down Owen Loney for dates all the time and leaving John Denby at the altar.

Ella listens and nods her head as we make our way down the road. She looks at the back of each beach house as we pass it.

"Are all these houses empty?" she asks. I can tell she's judging Maiden Rock, and I feel embarrassed.

"Most of them are closed up for the winter, except for the weekenders. There's Zoe's, where you live, and our house next door. There's the house at the preserve where Ben and his uncle live, the lobster pound where Owen Loney lives, the convent where the two sisters live. And Ms. Stillford's." I choke a bit on that last one.

"Now I get why my dad wanted to come here," Ella says.

"Why's that?" I ask.

"He writes gory crime novels, and this place is desolate."

"Where's your mom?" Ben asks.

"She lives in LA. She writes rom-coms for the movies. Why do you live with your uncle?"

"My parents are dead."

"Oh, yeah. For all I see my mom, she could be too."

I cringe and check Ben's reaction. I'm sure he'd rather have his parents living in LA instead of the Rook River Cemetery. But he shrugs and almost smiles.

Wonderful. So now they have that in common— dead or kind-of-dead mothers. And from what I could tell in Gusty's, her Dad is even less warm and fuzzy than Ben's uncle. Yet another reason for them to become best friends.

"Writing crime novels sounds cool," I say. I don't exactly mean it, but I'm trying to change the subject. I imagine Agatha Christie . . . but then I think of Ms. Stillford again, and my mind switches to *CSI*.

"So, maybe she's tied up in one of these houses," Ella says and points down the line.

I am considering this actually really brilliant possibility when a cry goes up from the searchers in the reeds along the edge of the Pool.

I hold my breath as a woman in a blue *RESCUE* coat leans over and picks up something. She waves at the others. It's small. I can't make it out. They gather like a fist, studying it. I imagine bad things. *Ms. Stillford's watch? Oh, no. Oh, no. Oh, no. Wha—?*

The searchers break apart and resume their walking. False alarm.

Ella looks at the Pool and says, "That's a pitiful lake."

The Pool isn't at its best at low tide. It's so shallow, you could wade into it, but you wouldn't want to, due to sharp shells, stranded marine life, and waterlogged trash.

"It's not a lake," I say. "It's a tide pool." But even though she doesn't know squat about tide pools, she may be right about Ms. Stillford being held in one of the houses.

"You know," I say to Ben, "she really could be in one of the summer houses."

I know Mom said she was going to check all the houses, but I decide, since we're here already, we should do it—look all around them.

"Yeah," Ben says. "He could have knocked on her door and thrown a bag over her head and put her in his pickup and tied her up in the cellar of any one of these."

"Or an upstairs bedroom," I add. I want her to be someplace nicer if she has to be tied up somewhere at all. Then, because the wheels are spinning in my head, I say, "Maybe I can get Mom to give us the keys to the houses."

Ben is hopping around in place. "Yeah, *and* the Abbotts', 'cause they border the marsh in the nature center. My uncle would probably hide her someplace closer to our house."

"Where he could walk to at night and not need the car or truck to take her *wild rice soup*," I practically shout.

"And," Ben says, "and, that is why he wants to search the marsh by himself. Because she's in a house near there."

"I sure hope it's not an Abbott," I say.

"What's an Abbott?" Ella tries to keep up with the conversation.

"They're the four abandoned houses at the other end of Mile Stretch Road."

Ben jogs ahead of me and Ella, opening mailboxes and sticking his nose in each one.

"Don't mess with the mail," I yell.

"There isn't any mail," he yells back.

Of course there isn't.

A plastic bag blows across our path. Ella grabs it and turns it inside out then lets it go. "What's down there?" She points down the drive of #1 Mile Stretch Road.

"The convent," I say as I keep my eye on Ben.

"Like with nuns?" She almost laughs as she says it.

"Mmm-hmm. Our Lady of the Tides Catholic Convent. Only two nuns left."

"Two?"

"Just two."

"That's weird."

"They're . . . a little weird."

Ella kicks over a piece of driftwood near the convent mailbox. A million tiny bugs swarm in the wood's crevices. Meanwhile, Ben has his head in the convent trash bins, rummaging like a gigantic raccoon.

At first I want to stop him but then I remember that they find evidence in the trash on *CSI* all the time. Instead, I hurry toward him.

"Oh, man. Look at this!" Ben pulls an empty, waxy-white, fifty-pound bag out of the trash. Across the front, it says *Mexican Bat Guano.* He thrusts it at Ella like he's won it for her at the carnival at Old Orchard Beach.

"Ick, I don't want that." She wrinkles her nose and backs up.

"You know what this is, don't you?" Ben says.

"An empty old stinky bag."

"It's bat poop. Bat *guano.* My uncle uses it for

fertilizer." Ben is clearly proud of his very specific gardening knowledge.

I look in the trash bins. "My mom's going to flip"

"Why?" Ella says. "Is bat guano illegal?"

"Paper mixed with glass and garbage." I pick a few things out of the trash bin, then throw them back. "They're supposed to separate. Mom's told them a hundred times."

"There's some cool stuff in here." Ben starts pulling things up from deep within the bins—a broken screwdriver, a cracked rubber hose. "This is gross," he says, but he keeps doing it. Crumpled potato chip bags, cupcake wrappers, at least twenty empty cat food cans.

Ella leans over the pile. "They have cats?"

"Oh, yeah." I try to count them from memory and stop at fifteen.

Ella looks closer. "Are they . . . fat?

"The cats?" I ask.

"The nuns." She looks at me like I am being purposely stupid, which I am.

Ella picks up a Suzie Q cupcake wrapper as if it's contaminated. "They don't exactly eat healthy."

"Sister Rosie is kind of a . . . chunk," Ben says. He shrugs his shoulders like he should get credit for not saying *fat*.

I'm about to give him a Ms. Stillford–style "watch yourself" look when we hear the convent van engine rev up. I immediately feel weird about going through the nuns' trash. It's embarrassing to see what they eat.

"Throw it all back in the bin, *now*," I yell.

A second later, the van barrels around the curve of the driveway, moving in our direction at a fierce pace. We jump back as it screeches to a halt in front of us.

The front windows power down simultaneously and two black-and-white nun heads appear. Sister Rosie is driving, as usual. I think about her promise to Mom and wonder if she only intends to keep it when she thinks Mom's watching. Her sweet, round face with its twinkly eyes makes me believe she really wants to comply but she just loves to drive fast.

The passenger, Sister Ethel, wears her typical somber look. Her face is wrinkled like an apple-head doll with two cloves for eyes.

Sister Rosie leans out excitedly and says, "Hello, dears. I know. I know. I know. Separate. We must start separating."

"We're on a search party," I say, "looking for clues about Ms. Stillford."

"Oh, yes. We heard. How worrisome." Sister Rosie makes a sad face. "Let's hope she's just taken a little vacation."

"Who is your friend, Quinnie?" asks Sister Ethel.

"This is Mar—*Ella* Philpotts. She and her dad are living in number nine while the Buttermans are in Scotland." Ella steps forward like the nuns are a curiosity. "This is Sister Rosie," I say and point to the driver. "And this is Sister Ethel."

Then Ella surprises me again. "I thought nuns were supposed to have saint names."

Sister Rosie doesn't miss a beat. "Oh, but we do. Rosie is short for Saint Maria Giuseppe Rossello, and Ethel is short for Saint Ethelburga of Barking."

Sister Ethel leans out the passenger window and extends her thin, wrinkled hand to Ella. "Welcome to Maiden Rock, Ella. Like Ella Marvell, I presume?"

I'm shocked by this, but not as much as Ella is. She leans forward and rests her hand lightly on the fender. "Yes, Sister. In her *Trouble* period, or maybe her *One and Only* period."

While I'm wondering how Sister Ethel knows squat about the uncontested queen of 1960s rhythm and blues, something happens that I will never forget, ever, in my whole life. Sister Ethel breaks into song.

"*Trouble hanging 'round me.*"

If that wasn't enough, Sister Rosie leans over and joins in.

"*Knocking at my door.*"

The next thing I know, Ella is singing with them. "*I give up a little but, yeah, yeah . . . But you always want me more.*"

Ben's grimacing like he's had bamboo shards shoved under his fingernails. Ella and the nuns continue to yowl. I have no clue whether this sounds anything like the real song.

Then Sister Ethel pats Ella's hand and says, "Well, we're off to Walmart for cat food."

"Quinnie," says Sister Rosie, "you must keep us posted on any news about Blythe. And tell your mother to let us know if there is anything we can do."

The only thing I can think to say is, "You could separate," but before I get it out, Sister Rosie guns the engine. I manage to yell, "Slow down, sisters," as they leave a dust swirl behind them.

"Ethel Burger of Dogby?" Ella asks.

"Ethelburga of Barking," I say.

"Whoa," Ella says. "Maine is crazy."

18

Ben, Ella, and I turn around and head south on Mile Stretch Road. You'd think we'd be jabbering about the sisters singing, but we're not. We're all in our own worlds. Ben's attention span is usually as short as a match burn, but he keeps sneaking looks at Ella like he's replaying the performance. I assume Ella is thinking about saint names since there's a small smile at the corners of her mouth.

Me? I'm thinking about searching all the houses along the beach.

"Hey," Ella says, "there are cars up there." She points up the road toward our and Zoe's houses.

"That's Zoe's house—your house. Don't you know your own car?" I say.

"We didn't have a car until this morning." She shrugs. "It's leased or something."

"Don't people own cars in New York?" Ben asks.

Now he's interested in NYC traffic.

"Mostly taxis," she says. "There's no place to park."

"Come on," I say, and I run around number two. I check the door, the windows. I go up on the porch on the beachside and look in. All the furniture is covered with sheets. Looks like it's untouched. "She's not here," I yell.

Ben is ahead of me at number three. He's stacking cinder blocks, climbing on them and looking in the windows. "This one is closed up tight," he calls out.

Ella tackles number four. "This one has boarded-over windows."

"Those are storm shutters," I say.

"I can't see a thing," she calls.

"Check if the door's locked," I say.

All the houses up to Zoe's house look undisturbed.

When we reach number nine, Ella's dad is unpacking the car. He mumbles something to himself as he carries in a box.

"Don't even ask," she says. "He's in the zone."

I don't ask.

"He's writing a novel," Ella continues.

"While he walks around?"

"Yep. He goes into the zone pretty much anywhere, and he just starts talking a story to himself."

I watch him nearly stumble on the steps but keep mumbling. I hope he isn't brainstorming a crime story about Ms. Stillford.

As we pass my house, I can see Mom though her office window. She's pacing and gesturing as she talks on her cell. She gives us a short, choppy wave.

We run around each of the houses until the end of the road. Ben's the quickest. He climbs and jumps and tugs at doors and yells to us, "Not this one! Nope!"

"He's really athletic," Ella says.

* * *

The four Abbott houses sit across the road from the ocean, perched on the edge of the marsh. Just looking at them gives me a feeling of spider legs on the back of my neck. I shudder to think that Ms. Stillford might be in one of them.

"Goth," Ella says, twisting strands of hair into a knot.

"The Abbotts," Ben whispers like he's describing something unholy.

I cringe. "Your uncle could sneak here from your house around the back of the marsh."

Something the size of a crow swishes overhead, and Ben and I duck. Ella shrieks and clutches Ben's arm. "What was that?" she gasps. Ben stands a little straighter.

I brush the top of my hair and see the culprit perch on the rooftop of Horror House. "Just a martin. They're swoopers."

"I thought it was a monster-sized bat," Ella says.

"Totally," Ben says.

"Like you can't tell a bird from a bat, all of a sudden," I say to Ben, but he doesn't hear me. He's concentrating on standing up straight since his arm is needed.

We stare at the dreary dumps that could be Ms. Stillford's prison. The wet wind blows against our jackets.

"Why don't they tear them down?" Ella asks. She's shivering.

"The Abbott family won't let the city touch them," I say.

"My uncle says an Abbott died in each one of them." Ben grabs his throat and pretends to choke himself. "They're like shrines or something."

"Shrines!" Ella gasps. "Sick."

Ben gets into it. "People say they're haunted."

"What people?" Ella asks.

"You know, old people around town." Ben has no idea. He's just telling it like he tells it to summer kids.

"My mom says they should be torn down for more rentals," I say. Thinking about the debate surrounding the houses reminds me that Ms. Stillford offered to make signs and picket outside the Abbotts with me for historic preservation. Now she might be tied up inside one of them.

The rusty metal wind chime on the porch of Abbott #1 jangles. I don't know how it hangs on.

"So . . . are we going in?" Ella asks.

Ben and I look at each other. I know we are both thinking of that Halloween when the floorboards under us gave way and Zoe and I fell through to our waists and Ben had to pull us out. That was the night we gave Abbot #1 the name Horror House.

"It's dangerous," Ben says. "No matter where you walk, it could collapse, and you'd fall into a pile of splintery boards with rusty nails sticking out."

Beyond the Abbotts, I see a team of searchers coming our way, whacking the reeds along the edge of the marsh with sticks. I wonder if John Denby is among them.

"I don't see how she could be in there," Ella says.

"But if there is any chance she is," I say, "I'm going in."

* * *

I touch the blistered paint covering Abbott #1 with my right hand. When I turn the corner at the back of the house, I can see across the marsh toward the nature center. The searchers are headed in that direction. They didn't even come near the Abbotts. I wonder if John Denby talked them out of it.

I put my fingertips on the railing of the rickety porch that hangs off the back of the house and start up the steps. My foot tells me how weak they are.

"Be careful," I say over my shoulder. "And don't pull too hard on the railing. It's about ready to fall off."

Behind me, I hear Ben say, "I'll go first. Hang on to me."

I summon the willpower to shake off the sound of Ben crushing on Ella. This is about finding Ms. Stillford, I tell myself, not about being jealous of Mariella Philpotts.

"I should have worn different shoes," Ella says.

My immediate thought is "Ya think?" but I don't say it.

I inch across the porch until I can look into the wreck of a kitchen. For as long as I can remember, Abbott #1 has been a place for summer kids to smoke and drink beer. In the last few years, summer people have helped themselves to crystal doorknobs and carved wall panels too, even though *PRIVATE NO TRESSPASSING* signs are plastered everywhere. Last spring, Mom sent old Miss Abbott a letter threatening to have all four houses officially condemned if she didn't either fix them up or tear them down. Horror House is in really bad shape, but it might be the perfect place to secret away a hostage.

My heart breaks a little for the house. I scan the planks for holes, potential breaks, possible places where my foot could plunge through. I gingerly put my weight on the most solid-looking board, then behind me I hear:

"Hey!"

Not a scared *hey*. A surprised *hey*. Maybe a slightly-incensed *hey*.

I turn and see Ben scoop Ella up and carry her across the porch. It's quick. His cheeks are red.

"Okay," Ella says. "Not necessary."

I'll say. *Ms. Stillford. Ms. Stillford.* I keep repeating it over and over.

Once I'm inside the kitchen, I grasp the amount of devastation. The floor has huge gaping holes with splintered edges. Only half of the stairway remains. The top steps hang suspended, trailing down into thin air. A hole in the roof that I've never seen before has let the Maine weather in with a vengeance.

"Back up," I say, my voice trembling.

"Holy smokes," Ben says when he sees the interior. "We've got to get out of here."

I hear a cracking sound, and Ella screams.

I turn and see her foot buried ankle-deep in the floor. She balances on her free leg with her knee slightly bent. Ben drops to his knees and crawls slowly towards her, the boards groaning beneath him. Ella stares at me with frightened eyes underneath her sparkly green lids.

"Don't move," I say.

Ben works to get Ella's foot out of her shoe so she can back away. Then he struggles to release the shoe from the jaws of the splintered floor.

Ella raises her arms like she expects to be picked up and carried out, but Ben is already three steps across the porch, holding her shoe and extending his hand to help her onto the solid ground.

I sprint across the creaky porch and take a deep breath when my feet reach the backyard. "Ms. Stillford can't be in there," I say.

"No kidding," Ben agrees.

I look back at the porch again. Ground-out cigarette butts litter the far edge. I'm about to go over and look at them when Ben and Ella yell "Don't!" in unison.

I cross the porch anyway. *Creak. Squeak. Creak. Crack.* The butts are fresh—as in *not* from summer kids. I drop them into one of the plastic baggies Mom gave me.

"What is it?" Ella says.

"Evidence," I yell back.

When I'm back on the ground, I give Ben the baggie. While he and Ella debate how fresh the cigarettes are, I look out into the marsh and see trampled weeds and reeds. It looks like more than one person has been here. Recently.

"That's a path," I say. "It may go to the nature center. . . . I mean, where else?"

Ben is starting to go pale. "My uncle doesn't smoke. Not cigarettes, not a pipe, not anything."

I tell Ben and Ella to wait, and I take off down the path. But instead of going to the nature center, it snakes through the damp edges of the marsh. Every once in a while, the path stops and widens as if its maker turned in circles. I round a patch of knee-high bushes and turn in a circle myself. It's nothing but marsh.

Eventually, the trampled plant life leads back to Horror House, where Ella and Ben are waiting.

"The path doesn't go anywhere," I say. Ben looks relieved. "But it's fresh."

19

We head back up Mile Stretch Road, toward Gusty's, to report our findings. All of a sudden, Ella is full of information. She's yakking on about her dad's books and things she learned from him about crime investigations and what some fictional detective named Monroe Spalding would do. Ella's talk is not really about Ms. Stillford. Why would it be? It's about showing off how much she knows.

"You should send the cigarette butts to a forensics lab for DNA testing—for lip prints in addition to finger prints. In *Bloody Footprints*, Monroe Spalding used genetic DNA testing to determine that the sweat on a scarf used to strangle the victim belonged to a female."

Back at Gusty's, Mom wields a clipboard and a whistle. She's wearing a blue *RESCUE* jacket that is three sizes too big for her—I guess she was the last person to reach the box.

Vreeeee! She gives the whistle a full bleat. "All right, everybody. *Quiet.*" Chair legs scrape, people finish their conversations. "Let's have reports. Group one?"

A man I recognize as a teacher from Rook River High School speaks up. "We had the harbor area, yacht club, lobster pound, grocery store, B&B, post office. Nothing. Mr. Loney didn't want us inside the pound for sanitary reasons. Said the lady never went in there, so we skipped it."

I look around for Owen Loney. He isn't there. I shoot Ben my "I told you so" expression and catch him looking at Ella.

"Fine," Mom says. "I'll talk to Mr. Loney and get that done. What about group two?"

Officer Dobson walks to the front of the room and edges Mom to the side. "Group two cordoned off the lighthouse and Maiden Rock historical marker location, set up containment, divided the location into sectors, and moved through each, meticulously examining the area for footprints, broken branches, and the like."

OMG. My concentration is totally blown. I didn't check for footprints.

"In sector 4A," Dobson continues, "the west side of the lighthouse, we observed, collected, and bagged this."

Dobson raises his arm. A group gasp sucks the air out of the room. A plastic baggie containing a dark brownish-black wad of something swings from his hand.

Mom grabs the baggie from Officer Dobson. "What is this?" she says, clearly irritated she hasn't seen the evidence until now.

"An item of apparel. A scarf."

"I'll take it to the lab in Rook River. Thank you." Mom turns the baggie over and runs her fingers across the surface of the bag. "Anything else?"

Dobson laughs. "That's not enough?" He looks across the group. "Anybody else find anything?"

Silence.

Dobson turns to Mom. "I've already tagged the item in accordance with the search-and-rescue protocol. You'll see the pertinent information there on the bag, including the date and time found and my name as search team leader."

A storm gathers on Mom's face, but she quells it. "Anyone else, in any of the search teams, find anything?"

A woman in a properly-fitting *RESCUE* jacket speaks up. "Our team had the area immediately south of the Maiden Rock historical marker, the one with the convent on it. We searched from the beach through the woods and up to the road. The grounds around the building are pretty overgrown, so it's hard to tell if anything looks unusual down there. And if you don't know already, there're quite a few cats around that place, and I think they're using the beach as a litter box." She wrinkles her nose. "The sisters came out and gave us cups of hot chocolate. We asked them if they'd seen anything unusual, and they said they hadn't. Before we left, they told us they were going to Walmart in Rook River for cat food."

The crowd laughs like a bunch of bobbleheads on a bumpy road.

Mom looks over the group and her eyes fall on me.

"How about your team, Quinnie?"

Ben starts to step forward, but I move past him toward the front and hand Mom the baggie. "We found the cigarette butts on the back porch of Abbott #1, and we found a new path trampled in the marsh back there."

People in the crowd press forward to get a look at the baggie. Dobson reaches for the cigarette butts, and Mom pivots so they're beyond his reach.

"Excellent, Quinnie. As soon as we break up here, you can take me to the spot, and I'll examine the area further. Did you see footprints?"

"No," I say so softly that she leans forward. "I didn't."

It's not exactly a lie. I didn't see any footprints. The problem is that I didn't look, either. I feel rotten. I was prepared to jump up and scream, "Look what I found!" Instead, I may have to admit that while walking all around the Abbott, I might have trampled over valuable evidence.

Mom takes this as regret that I didn't find any. I can tell. She hurries to say, "It's fine. Officer Dobson's group didn't observe any footprints either . . . or I'm sure he would have let us know, being so thorough and all. But your discovery warrants a further search."

* * *

Mom tells all of the searchers to report to the Abbotts and wait for her. Then the four of us pile into her sheriff's car and head there. Ella's in the middle-back, between me and Ben, studying the perp-barrier. Unintelligible squawks blast from the radio periodically.

I think Ben's about to explain the reason for the barrier, but Ella cuts him off and says, "My dad would really like this ride."

Mom pipes up helpfully from the front seat. "Mariella, you can tell him I will give him a neighborhood law enforcement familiarization ride in the squad any time he wants . . . Well, when this has all calmed down."

"Thanks," Ella says. "Cool. And it's Ella."

"Okay, then. Ella." I see Mom study her in the rearview mirror, wondering if this new girl is going to be a brat or if she's just confident.

When we get to Horror House, Mom has me show her exactly where I found the cigarette butts and the fresh path. Then she gives the teams instructions to "comb the area" and to "watch for footprints" and to "use a crosshatch pattern from behind the Abbotts all the way to the nature center." John Denby offers to help, but Mom tells him to meet her at the nature center. I watch her whisper to a man in a blue *RESCUE* coat.

"I want you to go home now," she tells me.

I can barely see though my watery eyes. "Is it because you think I wrecked the footprints?"

"No, honey. It's because you found something significant, and that marsh is no place for you right now. They have to do their search."

"She's alive, Mom."

"Oh, Quinn." She straightens my hair with her

fingertips and wipes the tears off my cheek. "I've been visualizing her safe and sound, and my instincts tell me she's going to be okay."

* * *

Mom tells me, Ben, and Ella to go back to our house. She adds that Ben should not go home until she calls him. For once, Ben isn't hungry. We don't even put on the TV. Ella tries to tell us about how in her dad's book, *Dark Observer*, the footprints were man-sized but made by a woman wearing her husband's boots. Calls come in to the sheriff's phone in the next room. Messages broadcast through the house because the speaker is turned up.

Beep. "This is Virginia Stark from Wooster. I think I saw the lady you are looking for in the Zippy Mart here."

Beep. "This is Joe Maroni. I'm staying at the Lake Champlain resort, and I think maybe the woman you're looking for is staying here too. Room three-one-four."

Beep. Beep. Beep. It goes on and on. She's been seen in Burlington, Vermont; Fryeburg, Maine; Concord, New Hampshire; and Amherst, Massachusetts, to name a few places.

Eventually, another phone rings—Ella's. Her ringtone is "Trouble," of course.

"My dad wants me home. I have to go unpack my room," she says. "But I can come back."

Just then, Mom calls my cell. As I raise it to my ear, I think, *Don't be bad news, don't be bad news, don't be bad news.*

"It's okay, Quinnie. We haven't found a thing. Relax. I'm just calling to tell you to send Ben home. Dad will be there with dinner soon."

I say good-bye to Ben and Ella. As she's leaving, Ella says again, "I can come back if you want."

If she were Zoe, there'd be no question. In fact, Zoe wouldn't have to ask. She'd just come back as soon as she could. But she's not Zoe, she's Ella, and I really don't want Ella to be with me. I don't really want anyone to be with me right now.

"Nah, it's okay. My dad will be home soon, and my mom."

She shrugs, nods like she understands, and jams her hands into her hoodie pockets.

Ben says, "Bye, Ella."

She tells Ben, "Yeah, bye," but she keeps looking at me. And I like her a little better for that.

It's five o'clock and getting dark in the house, so I walk around the main floor, flicking on light switches. I pick up a bowl of shells from the dining room table and blow at the dust ring under it. I straighten the stack of magazine we pulled apart looking for a maritime map. I pick up my phone to Google "maritime maps of Maine."

My phone pings a text arrival. It must be Ben. But when I look at it, I don't recognize the sender's number.

The cleverest lie is the one that is closest to the truth.

What? I start looking around, like something in my immediate area will tell me who sent the text. Then I think about its meaning. The smartest lie is almost the truth. Okay. So what?

This must be from Ella, I think. Another one of her Monroe Spalding things. Ha, ha.

I go up to my parents' bedroom, at the front of the house, and look out their window. The marsh starts near the intersection by our house, but it's dark enough now that I can't make out anything. Maybe they've stopped for the night.

At six, Dad calls to say he's closing Gusty's and bringing home chowder.

I set the table.

At six thirty, Mom straggles in, stomping dirt off her shoes on the front rug and shaking her head.

"Anything, Mom?"

"Nothing," she says as she peels off her coat and walks to the kitchen. "We'll start again tomorrow in the marsh and then spread out into Becker's Woods." She tosses my baggie and Officer Dobson's baggie onto the table. "Dobson'll lead the search groups tomorrow while I take these to the lab."

"Can I look at the scarf?" I touch the edge of the bag.

"Yes. But don't take it out."

"I know. I know. It's evidence."

I open the plastic bag with the scarf. Muddy. Mostly black. Silky. Shredded threads with no color left.

"Can I touch it?"

"Probably shouldn't, honey."

Springsteen goes off. Mom digs into her pockets.

I raise the baggie to my nose. It smells like rotting seaweed. "How could it get so gross in two days?"

"Just a minute . . ." Mom hates to miss a call. She digs and digs until Springsteen finally shuts up.

"Dang. Missed it."

"I don't think this is the scarf she wore the other day," I say and wish it to be true.

"Nah." Mom waves at the baggie in disgust. "Whatever *that* is has been out in the elements much longer than a couple days. But I'll take it to the lab anyway. Dad didn't bring any food yet?"

"Nope, not yet."

"Mom, can you get DNA off lip prints on a cigarette?"

"Well, there's something called *touch DNA*, where you can find DNA in grime and oil in fingerprints and tears and sweat, but there have to be human cells left behind to—"

I can't hear all of what she's saying because she starts walking down the hall. I follow her to her office, where she sits at her sheriff's desk and opens a drawer.

20

The front door opens and a cold breeze follows Dad into the house. He looks tired.

"If this keeps up, I'm going to have to place special orders. I'm running out of food and supplies," he says.

"Heck of a way to have a good sales day," says Mom.

"I'll say. But what do you think, Margaret? Should I place a big order?"

"How should I know, Gus?" Mom says it a little sharper than Dad deserves.

Dad grumbles and trudges upstairs. Mom leans her elbows on her desk and rubs her eyes.

"Sorry!" she yells over her shoulder, loud enough to catch Dad halfway up.

"I'll figure it out," he calls back down.

"Mom?"

"What, Quinnie?" She starts shuffling through a different drawer.

"Did you talk to John Denby?"

"I've lost something. I can't find the number for the lab. As soon as I find it, I'm going to bed. Got to get up early tomorrow."

"It's only eight o'clock," I say.

"Yes, and I have"—she switches to her file cabinet—"a big day tomorrow."

I put my hand on her shoulder. "Your instincts are right, Mom. We're going to find her."

"I know we are. We are going to do our very best to find her."

She finds the paper with the lab number in a third drawer and punches it into her phone's contact list, backspacing and muttering the whole time.

"Mom," I say, "did you talk to John Denby?"

"I did, and he had some questions."

"Shouldn't you have been the one asking him questions?"

"I was. I took his statement."

"Did he deny it?"

"Yes, he denied having anything to do with Blythe's disappearance. And he said he was out and about doing all of his normal activities every day of the last seven days. He's not happy with me, but"—she takes a deep breath—"that just comes along with the job. I have to do what I have to do."

"So, he's a suspect?"

"I would say . . . I haven't eliminated him as a suspect. But he is not a prime suspect by any means."

"Did you ask him about his clean pickup truck?"

"I did," Mom says. "He said he cleaned it up to get a trade-in price on it."

"That's the same as he told Ben."

"He says he can give me the name of the man he talked to at the dealership. That pretty much makes it impossible for him to drive to Houlton. I told him not to go anywhere but really, where's he going to go?"

"You'll watch him?"

"No."

I sink down into a guest chair. John Denby has an alibi.

I'm a little swayed by it.

"Mom?"

"Yes?"

"Tomorrow, when you go to Rook River to the lab, will you give me your keys to the houses so we can check them inside?"

She swivels around to face me and sighs. "I can't, Quinnie."

"Why not?" It almost comes out as a whine, but I get control of it midway through and twist it back into a calm question.

"Two reasons. First, it wouldn't be safe for you to do it. And second, the only people authorized to enter those premises are the agents of law enforcement or fire and rescue. And the rental agent. That's me and me." She leans back in her chair like she has more to say and is considering how to say it. "Besides, you're not qualified to do a proper search."

It comes out in whisper of finality, like she wants to get me out of the investigation.

"But I'm the one who told you she was kidnapped."

"Yes, but it was Blythe's letter that persuaded me something was actually wrong. We're here. It's serious. And you're a child—not a child-child, but you know what I mean. I can't have you in the middle of this. It wouldn't be professional—"

"Professional!" I lose it.

"Or *safe*."

I can feel a rage coming on, but I don't fume or flail. I don't stomp or scream. I say, "What *do* I get to do? I have to do something." The first part may be a question, but the second is a fact.

"I've been thinking about that," she says, "and one thing you can do is call back all the people who left messages and record their statements. I'll give you a list of questions to ask, and you record the answers on the phone. That way I can listen to everything they say."

"Like something a stupid computer could do."

She closes the file on her desk and stands up. "I'm going to ignore that. And I'm going to go up to bed."

"Mom?"

She pauses. "What?"

"What questions did Ben's uncle John have?"

"I can't tell you, Quinn. It's part of the official investigation file. I'll just say that he had many of the same questions we all have."

"Does that mean he suspects Owen Loney too?"

"No! Enough, Quinnie. Enough."

I follow her up the stairs. Before she closes her bedroom door she says, "Tomorrow, Quinn, and until this is over, stay away from Blythe's house and grounds. Understand?"

"Fine," I say, but I don't mean it one bit.

"Let me put it this way: if Blythe has been kidnapped, and you interfere with the crime scene, that could be obstruction of justice."

"I get it. I get it," I yell. And the reality blooms that looking for Ms. Stillford might turn me into a criminal. And drag Ben along with me.

I expect Mom to start threatening me with jail time, but then the phone sings.

"Hello? Yes? Yes, Chief."

I hover, listening to her conversation until she walks back down to her office and shuts the door.

21

Clothes are strewn around my room, and the bed hasn't been made in four days. The lights from the top floor of the convent are already blasting through my window.

I refuse to believe she's in the marsh.

I keep going over it in my mind. If Ms. Stillford isn't being held in a house along Mile Stretch Road—and she for sure isn't at Horror House—she has to be somewhere very close to home. How do I know this? Because I have good instincts, like Mom. It's in my DNA.

My phone pings with another text message. It's from the same unfamiliar number.

The fact that doesn't fit is the one that matters most.

Now I'm sure it's Ella. It has to be more Monroe Spalding. But still, what if it's from Ms. Stillford? No. She'd text, *HELP I've been kidnapped*. Her call number would come up on my phone. Is it from her kidnapper? Is this some kind of sicko—

Knock-knock. "Quinnie?"

It's Mom. I'm not sure why, but I slip my phone under the covers before she opens the door.

"The chief of police from Portland just called. He says he's sending us ten additional searchers for tomorrow. I thought you'd like to know."

"Thanks. That's good."

"Yes. It is. But I'll still be going to the lab tomorrow with the scarf and the cigarette butts." She opens the door a little wider and leans against the doorframe. "One of these days you have to start school—"

"*Mom—*"

"I know. I know. But Ben's going back to school tomorrow, and I thought maybe you and Mariella—Ella—could get together here, at our house, and just talk about a book you've both read. How's that? It's something."

I'd forgotten all about school. Well, not really. I just hoped Mom had forgotten about it. Guess not.

"Okay."

"Good night. I love you," Mom says. She doesn't move.

"I love you too," I say because I know that's what she wants to hear. And I think about how Ms.

Stillford always says, "Name the feelings." So I add, "But I'm mad at you."

"I understand," she says and shuts the door.

I pull my phone out from under the covers and stare at the text message:

The fact that doesn't fit is the one that matters most.

If this is from Ella, and if it's from one of her dad's books, maybe I should check out that book.

I read the text again and concentrate on what it means. Which fact doesn't fit? That Owen Loney wouldn't let the searchers in the pound? No, that actually fits with *him* being the kidnapper. That John Denby wanted to search alone? No, that fits with him being the kidnapper. The cigarette butts? That doesn't fit with Owen Loney or John Denby because they don't smoke. Is that it? What am I looking for—the profile for *being* the kidnapper or the profile for *not being* the kidnapper?

And what *is* the cleverest lie? That John Denby cleaned his pickup for a trade-in quote? It may be the truth. That Owen Loney says the *Blythe Spirit's* engine needed an odd part? That's too easy to check.

I give up trying to puzzle out the text messages and start planning my investigation for tomorrow. I'll ask the sisters at the convent about the nun in Ms. Stillford's letter; maybe they know some other nuns, some other convent between here and the border. Next, I'll stake out Owen Loney's Lobster Pound. He may be hiding her on his boat. Then I'll go back to Ms. Stillford's house.

My nerve withers when I think of how furious Mom will be if she finds out I'm doing any of this. But if she's going to shut me out, I guess I'm just going to have to run my own secret investigation to be sure *all* clues are followed, not just the official clues in the official investigation file. I'll investigate *all* suspects, even upstanding members of the community whose initials are O and L. No matter how mad this might make Mom, she'll be glad in the end that I did it. She'll thank me when Ms. Stillford is safe.

That's when I remember Ben's going to be in school, and I really will be alone in my investigation unless . . . annoying as it might be . . . I ask Ella to help me. That makes me think of Zoe, and that tightens a knot in my belly. When I need Zoe the most I've ever needed her, she's not here. Instead, Mariella Philpotts is sleeping in Zoe's room, with her crazy shoes, her green eye shadow, all that mouthing off about Monroe Spalding. At least she's interested enough to send me detective advice by anonymous text.

I pull my covers over my head to block out the convent lights and the noise of the surf. Every night of my life, as long as I can remember—until last Friday night—I've gone to bed knowing Ms. Stillford is a half-mile away. When I think about what might be happening to her, I want to rub my rock in my fingers, but I can't. I've lost it. A week ago, I would have looked for that silly rock until I found it. Now, I don't have time to worry about it.

* * *

Screech. Screech. Screech. A seagull squabble on the beach the next morning draws me out of bed.

I throw on my clothes from yesterday, drag a comb through my hair, and run downstairs.

There's a note on the kitchen table.

Quinnie,
    When I get home, you and Mariella should be having your book talk. Please let her know.
    See you at 3.
    Love, Mom

Three o'clock seems a lifetime away. I have so much to do. I need to get started. I'm anxious but I'm not afraid.

I walk into Mom's office.

I hesitate a second and consider the consequences of what I'm about to do. Then I shake them off and walk to her key drawer. The baggie marked *Stillford 6 Circle Lane* is on the top of the heap. There are two identical keys inside it. I slip one into my pocket— into the spot where my rock always used to be.

* * *

"We have to have a book talk this afternoon," I tell Ella when she answers the door. Today she's wearing even darker green shadow.

"Did they find her?" she asks. "What's a book talk?"

"No, they didn't find her, which is good considering where they were looking." It feels weird to be standing outside Zoe's door instead of going in. "My mom says if we can't start school, we should at least be talking about a book we both read."

"You want to come in and pick one out?"

"Maybe later. Now I have some investigating to do."

"Can we go up to my room first?"

I really don't have time, but I'm too curious about what she's done to Zoe's room to pass up a look. "Okay."

She waves me to follow her. "This way."

"I *think* I *know* the *way*."

The furniture is Zoe's, but entirely different stuff has exploded all over the room. Dark and sparkly stuff. Little nail polish bottles with shades like *Elfin Forest Green, Deep Space Blue, Moriarty Red.* Plastic bins filled with jewel-toned eye shadow pots. Coffee mugs blooming with makeup brush bouquets.

Ella's wearing jeans and a T-shirt with a spiraling psychedelic snail. I look at the shoes in her closet. Gold lamé ballet slippers, red patent leather pumps with glass heels, purple leopard-patterned slippers. She definitely has unusual taste in footwear. She picks silver sequined high-tops and grabs a hoodie with skulls on the front. I'm pretty sure Ben would be frightened by the sequins. He'd definitely stare at the skulls.

"I'm going to the convent to ask the sisters some questions."

"Cool," Ella says. "I'll go with you. I've never been inside a nunnery."

She didn't even give me a chance to ask her to come along.

"We won't go inside," I tell her. "They never let anyone past the front door. We'll stop at Gusty's and get a pie for them."

I try to sound casual when I bring up the mysterious messages. "Hey, I got your texts."

"What texts?"

I take out my phone and hand it to her. She reads them and hands it back to me. "Who are they from?"

"Uh, you. That's who."

"Nope. Not me. But it's not bad advice."

"It's kind of stupid advice if you ask me, since I don't know if it's a fact that doesn't fit the suspect or doesn't fit the non-suspect. And how do you know which lie is the cleverest if you don't know the truth?"

"Maybe you should ask your Ouija board." She thinks this is hilarious. Which it kind of is. But I'm a little irritated that she didn't admit to sending the texts. And if she really didn't send them, then I'm kind of freaking out. Nah, it must be Ella. Yeah, it's her. I'm sure it is.

22

Dad's happy to give us a pie for the sisters. He's in such a peppy mood with all the business that he's pouring free coffee for everyone in the café.

While I wait for him to box up the pie, I look around at the volunteers, chowing down before they start the search again. If Ms. Stillford saw this, I don't know what she'd think. She'd be happy so many people came out to look for her, but she'd be sad she had to be looked for.

It's chilly when Ella and I take off for the convent, and the warm pie box feels good against my fingertips. I hand Ella a copy of the letter from Ms. Stillford.

"Read this."

She walks and reads it, then reads a second time. I'm expecting her to say something but she doesn't.

"Do you think he was making her write it?" I finally ask.

"My dad would say she's trying to send a message."

Groan. Not Monroe Spalding again. "And he knows this how? Because he writes crime books? I mean, what do *you* think?"

"He says he puts himself in the position of each character and feels what they feel."

I'm beginning to think I made a mistake bringing Ella along. As we get closer to the convent, she goes on about how people are murdered and fingerprints and DNA and time of death determinations and rigor mortis. Apparently, Ella knows everything there is to know about solving crimes. I interrupt her. "So you know this because your dad is a crime writer?"

She doesn't miss a beat. "And I suppose you haven't learned anything from your mom the sheriff?"

"Yeah, I know some stuff from being a sheriff's daughter." I could say there's a big difference between real life and crime novels, but I decide to shake it off.

"Watch," I say. We round the bend in the weedy driveway, and the dilapidated convent building comes into sight. Blue and gray clouds roll over the roof, spilling around the chimneys.

"What?" Ella says.

"The sisters have some special nun way of knowing when someone is coming, whether you walk in from the street or up the beach. It's like nun-sense."

Ella rolls her eyes.

"I didn't make that up," I admit. "Ben did." But before she can take the opportunity to ask me anything about Ben, the sisters prove me right. The front door opens, and Sister Ethel sticks her head out.

"Hi ho!" she says. "Troubled weather night last night, eh?" She gives us a small, wrinkled smile.

"Troubled," Ella agrees, as pleased as she can be, until the bad odor registers on her face. Cats. Cat pee. A meowing chorus from all directions. Sister Ethel shoos away the cats who are trying to wipe their whiskers on her skirt. Spiro meanders among them.

"Here we are." Sister Rosie bustles through the door, nudging Sister Ethel aside. She carries two paper cups. "Autumn is in the air, don't you think, girls? The chill always makes me crave hot cocoa." She hands us each a drink. The sweet steam tickles my nose.

Cats keep arriving from every direction. At least thirty mill around the front yard. I look sideways at Ella. She's alternately trying to sneak a peek through the open door and looking back up the drive for an escape path. In the garden, rusty tools with rotted wooden handles lean on a bent wire birdcage. A wheelbarrow is flipped over at a cockamamie angle with stacks of empty, dark green plastic flowerpots next to it.

"Aren't you nice!" Sister Rosie twiddles her fingers in anticipation of the Gusty's pie.

"Hot out of the oven, Sister," I say, extending it. Sister Rosie reaches for the box with both hands. I don't let go. "But—I have a couple questions."

Sister Rosie drops her arms.

"It's about separating the paper and the plastic, isn't it?" says Sister Ethel. "Not throwing them in the bin together."

"We know," says Sister Rosie. "We need to say extra Hail Marys."

By this time, the cats have wandered into the house.

A loud crash sounds from somewhere inside the convent—like a vase falling off a shelf and smashing to smithereens. All four of us jump. "Oh! Those naughties," Sister Ethel says. "Rosie, go see to that mess. And shoo the cats out of the convent." She turns back to me. "You can tell your mother that I'm monitoring Sister Rosie's driving."

"That's not it, Sister," I say.

Her dark eyes narrow. "The lights, then. Maybe

in a week or so, we can cut back on the lights a bit."

"That would be good, but I have another question."

By this time, Sister Rosie has returned. She pushes her chubby face back into the conversation.

"Anything broken?" Ella asks.

"They knocked over a statue of Saint John the Baptist," Rosie says. "Not to worry. Nothing that superglue can't fix."

"We got a letter from Ms. Stillford saying she's in Canada."

The sisters start clapping, which makes their black sleeves flap like bat wings. "Wonderful! Great," Sister Rosie says.

"That's a relief," says Sister Ethel. "Thanks so much for letting us know. And thanks for the pie."

Sister Rosie reaches for the pie box, but I hold it back.

"We're not sure the letter is genuine," I say. "We think Ms. Stillford was forced to write it, and I think she is trying to tell us something in the letter."

The sisters look shocked.

"Sisters, I think she wants me to ask you about something."

"Why us?" Sister Ethel asks.

"Have you talked to Ms. Stillford recently?" I ask.

The sisters look at each other as if puzzled by the question. Then Sister Ethel says, "Only about the fund-raiser."

"Fund-raiser?" I didn't expect this.

Sister Rosie smiles. "Right. Blythe helped us design a tea to sell—to raise money for the convent."

This is all news to me.

Ella comes to life. "Herbal tea?"

"Yes, dear. A nice herbal tea," says Sister Rosie. "We call it Sanctity Tea. 'It's not only for relaxing, it's for giving.' *For. Giving.* Forgiving. Get it?"

"That's cool," Ella says. "Where do you sell it?"

Sister Rosie beams and says, "Online."

Okay, the two sisters are selling herbal tea on the Internet. It's interesting news, but I don't know how it helps me find Ms. Stillford.

"Did Ms. Stillford ever mention she had a nun for a relative?" I ask.

"A nun? No," Sister Rosie says. "Well, maybe. Let me think. I do recall her mentioning a nun once."

"I'm sure she's fine, dear," Sister Ethel says. "Blythe never tells a lie, not even a little snitch of one. If she says she's in Canada, then she's in Canada." She pulls Sister Rosie back through the door.

"Good-bye, dears," Sister Rosie calls out. The convent's large wooden door whooshes shut with such force that a weathered shutter from an upstairs window comes loose and topples the wheelbarrow below. Ella and I both scream. Cats scatter into the woods. The single wheel of the overturned wheelbarrow spins with a wonky *rrt . . . rrt . . . rrt.*

It's almost completely overcast now. A couple fearless cats continue to wander around the front of the convent. One of them starts snaking between my legs.

Suddenly, the door reopens. Sister Rosie reaches out and grabs the pie box from my hands.

"Bless you, dears," she says, and she ducks back inside.

23

Ella and I are on our way to Loney's Lobster Pound, neither of us talking, when Ella turns to me and says, "You lied."

"What?" I never lie, I think. Oh, wait. Yes, I do. I've become a horrific liar.

"You said they were *a little* weird. There's a difference between being *a little* weird and being . . . shut-the-front-door flakesters."

"Kind of cool flakesters, though, don't you think?" I say. "I mean, the whole selling-tea-on-the-Internet thing? I didn't think they knew anything about the Internet."

"Uh huh, and I am totally checking out that tea and telling all my friends in New York to buy some and support them."

"I'm sure my mom has no idea they're doing this. She'd probably find some reason why they shouldn't."

"Why would she care?" Ella says. "I thought she only cared about them recycling."

"Recycling, speeding, turning off the lights at night. But mostly, she wants a clean, orderly town with a future. When the monsignor told my mom he was considering selling the convent, she really wanted to make that happen. I mean, she's right. The convent is a wreck."

"A cat dump."

We thrash through the woods with me in the lead. "This way, Owen Loney won't see us coming if he's on his dock."

A couple times, Ella says, "Slow down," and I say, "Hurry up."

We peek out of the woods across the street from Miss Wickham's Bed & Breakfast. The winter shutters are in place, and all the rocking chairs are face down and lashed to the porch railings. I'm relieved to see there are no search teams around. We sprint over to the B&B's porch and crouch behind the chair bunker.

"*This* is town," I whisper. I point to each of the buildings. "That's the yacht club. It's closed for the winter . . ."

"Swanky," says Ella. "Not exactly what you think of when you hear the word *yacht*."

It's true. The Maiden Rock Yacht Club is a three-story wooden warehouse with the paint mostly worn off and hooks, chains, and hoists swinging from a third-story window.

Inside, though, are thirty small sailing skiffs, bedded down for the winter. And when their bright white-and-marine-blue stripes set sail around the Pool with a class of eight-year-old Junior Skippers, it's the happiest sight you'll ever see. Ben and I crashed one of those skiffs into the dock more than once. I am about to tell Ella the story, but I stop. I realize I want to keep my Ben stories to myself.

"That's Loney's Lobster Pound." I point to a gray building with a sturdy dock. A sign next to the door says:

MAIDEN ROCK POOLE LOBSTER POUND

LONEY LOBSTERMEN

PROPRIETORS SINCE 1918

Ella stretches her neck and takes it all in. Barrels of colored glass balls stand next to the door. A mountain of crookedly-stacked wood-and-mesh lobster traps fills the space between the pound and the dock. Buoys with Loney's distinctive green, yellow, and purple bands overflow from a bin next to the traps. Old truck tires crusted with salt are tied to the pillars that hold up the dock.

"Tires?" Ella asks.

"So the boat won't hit the dock."

The boat is gone, and Loney's pickup sits in its usual spot, in front of the weathered screen door.

I pivot on my knees and point behind us. "There's the grocery. It's closed for the winter . . . and up there, the last building you can see is the post office. It's closed, except when Mom's there."

I realize this porch is a near-perfect vantage point for the goings-on in the little town center.

"Let's check out the lobster pound," Ella urges.

"No! Owen Loney's on his run, and he'll be back any minute."

We settle down on Miss Wickham's porch, which shelters us from the wind. Ella picks at the fashion-frayed sleeve of her hoodie like she has something on her mind.

"Why are we tutored when Ben gets to go to real school?" she asks.

"His uncle won't pay for private tutoring, and Ben wants to go out for team sports anyway."

"Isn't going to school with people—with guys—better than being stuck out here all winter?"

Hmmm. How can I explain this? Years of wonderful experiences with Ms. Stillford flash through my mind. I choke up a little bit. "I like it. I love Ms. Stillford. She's a great teacher, and I hate . . . crowds of kids . . . and crappy school lunches . . . and mean girls and . . . my parents both work long hours . . . and it's hard to get back and forth . . . and I had Zoe."

"I don't mind tons of kids. But not mean girls. Guys, I like. But not jerky guys."

"You'll like Ms. Stillford, you'll see."

"I'm going to be bored to death."

"*Don't* say death."

"Sorry. Didn't mean it. Sorry. Sorry."

We wait. Absolutely nothing happens for thirty-three minutes except we watch the gulls play around the dock. Finally, we hear a boat motoring through the channel into the Pool. We huddle together and watch through the porch railing as Owen Loney jockeys the lobster boat in a tight turn and inches it against the bumpers. Gulls on the pylons take to the air, screeching their annoyance.

I study him for signs of something unusual. I've known this man my whole life. He was almost like an uncle. Now he frightens me. He could be a maniac psycho-killer lover kidnapper.

"What does that say on the boat?" Ella pops her head up, and I yank her down.

"*Blythe Spirit.* That's the name of the boat."

She looks at me with wide-open eyes framed with what I now know is *Elfin Forest Green* shadow. "Blythe Spirit? As in Blythe *Stillford* Spirit?"

Of course this would surprise Ella. But the town's had a long time to get used to it. It's part of Owen Loney's dedication to Ms. Stillford. Mom calls it "carrying a torch." I don't get that expression, but I get that he named the boat after her, which is the highest honor a fisherman can give someone.

Maybe it's not dedication or carrying a torch—it's *obsession.* He always offers her a ride. He always holds the door for her. He always brings her punch at the Fourth of July picnic. He plows her driveway after a snow. He shovels her walk. He fixes her flat tires.

"Okay, let's get serious. What are his patterns?" Ella's voice gets louder.

"Shhhh." I put my finger to my lips. "His patterns?"

"My dad says criminals all have patterns they live by. Actually, everyone has patterns. You can catch a criminal by studying their regular daily movements, then looking for variations."

"I already know that. That's why we need to know if he was missing for eight hours to drive to Houlton and back on Saturday for the postmark."

"If you're so smart," Ella says, "what's he doing now? Is it in his pattern? And when will he leave so we can get on that boat and find some evidence?"

I peek at the boat. He's swinging lobster-filled crates up onto the dock.

"He'll take all the lobsters inside and dump them in the tanks, then he'll clean the boat. After that, he'll go to Gusty's for lunch. Then he'll come back here to wait for the restaurant buyers."

"So we can snoop around while he's at lunch?"

"And since Mom won't be back from Rook River until three o'clock, we can go search Ms. Stillford's too."

Ella looks toward the pound and says, "Come on, Owen Loney, you nasty old kidnapper! Get a move on."

24

Owen Loney takes twenty-seven minutes to finish unloading the lobsters, spray down the boat, and drive away.

I open the pound's creaky screen door. Owen Loney never locks it. The smell of lobsters hits us in the face, and Ella gags. A long counter keeps customers away from the lobster tanks, but Ella and I can hear the clacking of claws against stainless steel. Handwritten signs advertise various sizes of lobster: *1 pound, 1 ¼ pound, 1 ½ pound, 1 ¾ pound, 2 pound, Higher.*

We slip behind the counter. The lobsters squirm and spider-leg over each other.

"What's with the red rubber bands?" Ella asks. "So they don't snap you when you hold them?"

"They're cannibals," I say. "If they weren't banded, they'd eat each other."

Ella shivers. "Sick."

The menu on the wall reads: *Steamed/Boiled/Picked. Ask for price by the day.*

Ella walks over to a wall with old-time photographs of men in fishing gear. Each has a small nameplate at the bottom. Every one of them has the last name Loney, but one in particular captures Ella's interest: *HASWELL LONEY, 1927–2006.* Haswell stands in front of the pound, wearing rubber overalls and grinning with a mouth full of broken teeth.

"Ben's uncle John says that Haswell was 'a mean old devil,'" I tell her.

"I guess that explains how the family has a kidnapper in it," Ella says.

"I guess."

"Where does he sleep?"

I point toward the far corner where a small doorway leads to stairs. "Up there."

I've never been up the stairs or even imagined what it would be like, but once Ella and I sprint to the top and look into the apartment, all I can say is, "Wow."

"It looks like Captain Jack Sparrow lives here," Ella says.

The room has a tiny kitchen in one corner and a bed in the other, along with hardwood floors, a massive braid rug, an oak table with a round top, hurricane lamps, a carved wooden pelican, a pipe stand, and a framed map of the coastline from 1936. Oh, and Owen Loney's bookcase—mysteries. I pull one off the shelf and flip it over. *Bracing and spectacular. Best nautical suspense novel of the year.* And another: *Heroism, madness, and savagery.*

Ella and I look at each other and laugh nervously.

"This place is neater than I thought it would be," I say.

Framed photographs crowd the top of the bookcase: Owen Loney and John Denby (and Ms. Stillford) in their high school senior class picture; Owen Loney with his parents and Ms. Stillford at the christening of the *Blythe Spirit* (Ms. Stillford holds the champagne bottle); Owen Loney on the *Blythe Spirit*, dressed as Santa Claus, tossing candy canes to me, Zoe, and Ben (Ms. Stillford stands next to us).

"This bedspread is serious work." Ella fingers the edge of a patchwork quilt. I point to the initials embroidered in the corner: *BS*.

"Ms. Stillford made this quilt."

"Do you think he stole it from her house?" Ella asks.

"Or maybe she gave to him . . . or made it for him," I say. I've never seen it before. Maybe there's a lot I don't know about Ms. Stillford.

Ella opens the closet and leans over.

"What are you doing?" I say.

"I'm looking through the dirty clothes basket."

I run to the window to be sure Owen Loney isn't coming. We'll never be able to explain what we're doing in his apartment, or worse, in his closet looking through his dirty clothes.

"Oh my gosh!" Ella springs up with a T-shirt in her hands. A dark, almost black spot stains the center—over the heart. "Blood."

"Are you sure it's not oil?" Not blood. Not blood.

"No. This looks like blood."

"Smell it," I say.

"I'm not going to smell it. You smell it. She's your teacher."

"Like I can recognize the smell of her blood. You've got glitter in your brain." I grab the shirt and touch the spot. It's dry. Of course it is. It has been days since he would have snatched Ms. Stillford. I scrape the edge of the stain with my fingernail. Flakes drift to the floor.

"Let's take it with us," Ella says and starts to roll it up.

"No! He'll know someone is onto him and then he'll do I-don't-know-what to her."

"Well, take a picture of it with your phone."

I select three wrong apps before the camera comes up. "Hold it up by the window so you can tell it's in this apartment," I say.

"Hurry, hurry," she says. "We have to search the boat."

I don't think more than thirty seconds pass before we are jumping onto the *Blythe Spirit*. Ella has no sea legs and lands on her butt in the first step. The boat lurches sideways and bumps against the dock. Ella's shoes spew glittery sparkles on the planking.

"Grab the gunwale," I yell.

"What's the gunwale?" she yells back.

"It's the railing, the edge, the ledge, the top of the little fence around the deck." I decide to just grab it myself.

"Oh, the gunwale."

There aren't many places to search on a lobster boat—a few compartments, some chests, the cockpit. But Ella starts thrashing through everything she can find. I try to imagine where Owen Loney might stash any incriminating evidence. Then I see a rolled-up, lumpy wad of canvas.

It has something long and weighty inside of it, like a five-pound mallet. Ella takes it from me and starts to unwrap it. At the same time, we hear a car turning off Mile Stretch Road, heading in our direction at a good clip. It has to be Owen Loney, coming back from Gusty's.

"We have to get out of here," I scream.

There is nowhere to hide. There is nowhere to run. Seconds are flying by. Owen Loney will come around in front of the yacht club any second, and we'll be standing in his boat in plain view. That's when I hear the splash and see two sparkled feet disappear over the edge of the boat. Ella is in the water, holding the tarp-wrapped evidence over her head. I have no time to consider alternatives. I go over after her.

And just in time. Another split second, and I would have been seen. Not by Owen Loney but by *Mom*! She is back and heading for the post office. No, she drives past the post office. She has to be going to Ms. Stillford's. I'm sure she checked at home and at Gusty's and didn't find me. Now she expects me to catch me at Ms. Stillford's, violating her order.

"Are you a good swimmer?" I pant.

Ella shakes her head but keeps the bundle high out of the water. We hang on the outboard side of the *Blythe Spirit*, trying to decide which way to go. We are sunk either way, because at that moment, Owen Loney's pickup rounds the bend.

25

My clothes and shoes are dragging me down. The deep channel from the Pool to the open Atlantic is swelled to high tide and swirling with strong currents.

If we try to swim through the channel, we'll never make it around to our beach. Even if we get to the open ocean, we'll be slammed against Maiden Rock like all those spinsters in the stories.

The water, which is too cold for swimming even in the summer, is getting harder and harder to yank our legs through. Ella and I grasp the *Blythe Spirit* anyway we can.

Worrying that Ms. Stillford's house key will come out of my pocket and sink, I lift my right leg as high as possible, trying to keep the pocket closed while I thrash around.

"What are you doing?" Ella says, spitting out salty water.

"Quiet," I say. "He'll hear you."

I don't think this can get any worse, but then it does. The gunwale above our heads serves as a perch for a trio of seagulls. They look down on us with cocked heads. One turns around and, yup, poops on Ella's hair.

No one can tread freezing water, wipe seagull poop out of her hair, and hold a heavy wad of canvas over her head all at once. At least Ella can't.

"Give me the canvas." I bob up and down, trying to take the bundle from her.

Ella surprises me with her calmness. She tips her head back into the water and shakes it, trying to free the white goo.

"You look beautiful," I say.

"I look better than you do," she says as she grabs the gunwale.

"I don't think so. You have white crap on your hair and green stripes running down you face."

We tread water for another couple minutes. I try to decide if Ella's lips are really turning blue. Mine are starting to feel numb. I realize we have to get out of this frigid water soon. Then Mom's car zooms by, heading toward home. At the same time, Owen Loney pushes open the screen door and walks toward the boat.

Ella and I exchange frantic looks and move as quietly as we can toward the end of the dock. As Owen Loney steps into the *Blythe Spirit*, it rocks, and we make a grab for the framework of lashed timbers that holds the dock up. The bitter-cold seawater bites my legs.

Ella grabs my hand and mouths, *My-phone-is-ringing-in-my-pocket!* She points down. *In-my-pocket!*

I mouth back, *I-can't-hear-it.*

She mouths, *I-can-feel-it.*

Of course, that makes me think about *my* phone. I hand the bundle back to Ella, who holds it over her head again, and pat myself down through the cold water. Key, yes. Phone, uh-oh! When did I last see it? Did I have it in the boat? I don't know. Did I have it in the pound? I must have—I took a picture in Owen Loney's apartment. Did I leave the phone there?

I look at Ella's lips again and know that she has to get out of the water right away. Except for the green stripes, her face is gray. Her hair is a mess of knotted ropes spotted with seagull goop. And her fingers are losing their grip on the wooden pillars.

If only Owen Loney would go back inside the pound.

But of course, he doesn't. He's grumbling to himself and chucking things around in the boat, making it lurch up and down. Then he does something unexpected. He starts the engine, casts off, and eases away from the dock. We watch him head into the channel, making a wake that throws us against the posts.

But at least he's gone and we can get out of the water.

Ella and I swim around the dock to the ladder near the lobster buoys. I take the canvas while Ella climbs up and then hand it to her. She pulls me up, and we collapse onto the planks, trying to take in what heat the air offers.

"We have to get out of here, now," I say, not making a move.

"I know." Ella lies flat as a sand dollar, unable to raise her voice.

The wind blows a wave of cold air through our bones, and we struggle to our feet. We both still have our shoes on. Stupid. We should have kicked them off when we got stuck in the water. But I'm happy to have them now.

There is no doubt in my mind about next steps. "I have to go back up to Owen Loney's apartment and find my phone, if he hasn't already found it."

"We're dripping wet," Ella says.

"I don't care. I have to have that phone. It's

bad enough that it's the third phone I've lost since Christmas. It's worse that I lost it at Owen Loney's."

"I know, I know. Do you want me to go with you?"

"No. You wait on Miss Wickham's porch, where you'll be out of the wind. I'll be right there. Then we'll go to Ms. Stillford's, where we can warm up and look for more clues."

Our shoes squish as we walk, and we leave big wet footprints on the dock. Ella looks over her shoulder as she heads to the B&B, keeping her eye on me until I open the door to Loney's Lobster Pound.

Either the daylight has faded or Owen Loney's turned off the lights, because it's much darker in here. I look to the door that leads upstairs, and it's shut. *Pulled shut.* That door is never shut. He knows. What if he has my phone? What if he saw the picture?

My legs are like lead. It takes all my energy to place my feet, one after the other, on the steps. I listen for the boat in case it's coming back into the channel. Nothing.

Pay attention and hurry up, I tell myself. Hope, hope, hope the phone is there, get it, and get out. I know I'm leaving wet footprints on the stairs, but at least they won't point a finger directly at me like my phone will. And if he stays away long enough, maybe they'll dry up.

I reach the landing and run to the spot where Ella and I took the picture. I scan the floor like a search-light from a lighthouse beacon. Nothing. Under the bed, dust wads but no phone. Under the bureau, no phone. Every surface, no phone. The laundry basket—empty!

He took his dirty laundry out to sea?

A distant glugging sound tells me a boat has entered the channel. My heart nearly leaps into the Pool. Halfway down the stairs, I bang my elbow and wince with pain. Outside the door, I stop to listen for the rumble of motor blades coming closer. Nothing. False alarm. Ella sees me coming and jumps up. We run up the street to Ms. Stillford's house. I reach into my wet pocket as we run. Feeling for the key. Yes.

26

There's no crime scene tape around the house, but I still don't want to disturb anything. That doesn't keep me from getting us two big towels to wrap around our shoulders. We sit on Ms. Stillford's living room floor with the canvas *thing* between us.

"Can you feel your toes?" I ask Ella.

She wiggles her toes.

"Your fingers?"

She fans the air with her hands.

"Your lips?"

She smacks them. "Still work."

I finger the corner of the rolled canvas bundle. "We have to look inside."

Ella points to a red tinge on the canvas. "Okay, but I'm pretty sure that stuff's blood."

If this were two days ago, I'd run home and thrust the bundle at Mom so she could put on surgical gloves, peel back the tarp, and take pictures. But I now know that if I do that, she'll ask me where I got it, and when I tell her, she'll be furious. Worse, she'll probably show it to Owen Loney, which will give him a big fat chance to explain it away.

Not today. The bundle is going to be part of the unofficial investigation until I can tie it to the shirt. And maybe we'll find something else here at Ms. Stillford's. If only I had my phone—I'd have pictures of the missing shirt.

Random images of wild eyes and a taped-shut mouth swim through my head. Before I know it, I've buried my face in my hands and started whimpering.

"Hey, Quinnie, it'll be okay," Ella says. "Hey. He loves her. Right?"

"This could be"—I start to say it out loud. "This could be"—then it dawns on me that Ella has her phone. "Can I see your phone?"

"It's dead, done, destroyed by the deep blue sea."

"I thought it rang underwater," I say.

"I think that was a muscle twitching in my leg."

I take a deep breath. "Okay, let's get this over with. Ready?"

I pull one corner of the tarp and feel something heavy clunking as it flips over and lands on the floor in a thud. We scream in unison.

"What is *that*?" Ella's eyes bulge.

"It's a gaff hook." I hear my voice as if I'm wearing earmuffs. A black iron tool with a swooping curved neck and barbed hook electrifies the space between us. "It's for snagging a lobster crate."

Ella shutters. "It looks like a fishing hook on steroids."

"It could do some damage," I say, staring at the large red stain on the tarp.

"Looks like it already has. Should we take it to your mom?"

I don't hesitate. "No. We should hide it for now."

"Are you sure?"

"Just until I can get the picture of his shirt off my phone and check this place for any Owen Loney kind of evidence."

"I don't know, Quinnie." Ella points at the gaff hook. "This could be—"

"My mom won't believe it unless we have more proof."

"Right. Okay. How do we do that?" Ella bites her hoodie string, "Monroe Spalding says, 'Always look beyond the obvious.'"

She's talking like one of those text messages again. "*Did* you send me those texts?" I ask her.

"I told you already," Ella says, "they're probably

from your Ouija board. Now let's hide this thing."

I get busy rewrapping the hook. "Let's bury it in the woods. But before we do, I want to sweep the house, the shed, and the garage."

"And put these towels back." Ella gives hers up.

* * *

We don't find anything Loney-like in the house, so we head to the potting shed. I keep thinking through every move I made since I had the phone in my hand by Owen Loney's window. I don't remember having it after that. Now it's probably in Loney's pocket.

The shed looks the same as when I last looked in it. I think.

"What are all these?" Ella looks at the shed's volumes of botany books.

I lean over the little seed starter pods. Each has two-leaf buds pushing out of the dirt.

"Wow, that's fast. These weren't up last Friday."

"What are they?"

I pick up the empty seed envelope. "It must be this stuff. Maypop."

Ella reads from an open book. "'*Passiflora incarnata*. Common name *passionflower* or *maypop*. The leaves and roots have a long history of use among

Native Americans. Tea makers have used maypop to treat insomnia, hysteria, and epilepsy. Maypop is also valued for its analgesic properties.'"

"Do you think this is what's in the sisters' tea? The one she helped them with?" I ask.

"Yeah, Sanctity Tea. 'It's not only for relaxing, it's for giving.'" Ella makes a face that almost looks like Sister Rosie, and I laugh. I laugh because I need something to laugh about.

We grab shovels from the shed and run deep into the woods beside the house, where we dig like mad, toss in the tarp and its creepy contents, and rake the soil over it—leaves and all. I mark a nearby tree with an X, and we return the shovels.

The sun has shifted to about two o'clock, and I know Mom is at home doing about ten different things, one of which is grumbling because Ella and I aren't sitting at the kitchen table discussing a book.

"Okay, we're supposed to be discussing a book. We need to go to my house and face the music."

"Yep, Springsteen," Ella says and looks at me like we're going to laugh some more.

I know we just nearly drowned together, and lost our phones together, and dug a secret hiding place in the woods together, but joking about Mom's Springsteen ringtone? I don't think so. Not yet.

27

Ella and I march up the steps and stand in Mom's office door. She's sitting at the sheriff's desk with her back to us, rifling through a thick pack of papers. She swivels her chair and looks at us and does a double take.

"What the heck happened to you two? I've been calling you. Why are you wet? Mariella, what's in your hair?"

"I lost my phone," I tell her.

She throws up her hands. "Quinn, that's what? The third one? Help me out here."

I'm almost glad the lost phone distracts her, because it gives me a chance to invent the lie of the century about where we've been.

Ella jumps in. "We were by the ocean, and a gull pooped on my head"—she gestures to her hair—"and I freaked and I jumped in the water, and while

I was there, I lost my phone and I freaked a second time, and Quinnie jumped in to help me, and now she's lost her phone." She takes a deep breath.

Mom looks at Ella like she isn't sure whether to believe a word of this or not.

Ella adds, "My dad is going to be so mad." She pauses. "Are you going to tell him?"

In an instant, Mom relaxes like she completely believes Ella's story. I can tell she's thinking about whether she should get involved in this or not.

Then she resumes pawing in her papers. "I'll let you handle this with your father yourself, Mariella. You guys get cleaned up. Quinnie can loan you some dry clothes." She turns to me. "Did you get the statements from the people who left the phone messages?"

"Not yet," I say. I don't make it sound like an apology, or like I forgot, or even like I'm defying her. I just say, "Not yet."

She gives me a look that says she knows I'm making a point.

"Did you find anything on the search this morning?" I ask.

"No, but I can't really talk about it," she says. She changes the subject in a hurry.

So that's the way it's going to be. Now I know I made the right decision about the gaff hook.

Sitting at our kitchen table, wearing my clothes, Ella looks pretty much like a Maiden Rocker. I think about the lie she just told my mom and I remember the text message. *The cleverest lie is the one that's closest to the truth.* Ella's lie was definitely closer to the truth than the whopper I was working on. But what made it great was that she asked Mom if Mom was going to tell on her.

If I had my phone, I'd send a message to the mysterious texter that says: *A good lie shifts the focus from the liar to the listener.*

This makes me wonder if I am thinking about Ms. Stillford's disappearance in entirely the wrong way.

* * *

Ella and I spend most of the hour between three and four trying to figure out a book we've both read. Mom comes in and takes pity on us and sends us to Gusty's for dinner. She says she has to meet a new real estate client. I'm not happy that she's meeting clients instead of searching for Ms. Stillford, but I'm learning that Mom's talent for multitasking isn't something she can turn off.

We go next door and listen at Ella's dad's office door. The keyboard is clicking at a snappy pace. Ella knocks and puts her ear to the door. "Dad?"

He yells from behind his office door, "In the zone."

She pulls at my sleeve. "Come on. He'll be in the zone all night."

* * *

We're heading for Gusty's when Ben charges up behind us, every inch of him sweaty-cute.

"Hey," he says, "the convent van is parked down by the Abbotts. What's up with that? And what's up with you not answering your phone, Q?"

He squints at Ella like he can tell something's different but he doesn't know what it is. She picks at her eyebrow, trying to cover up her naked eyelids.

"I lost my phone in Owen Loney's apartment after I used it to take a picture of his bloody shirt," I tell Ben. "Then we found a bloody gaff hook in his boat and buried it in the woods by Ms. Stillford's." I pause to see if he's paying attention.

"Whoa, whoa, whoa." He rakes his hands through his hair. "What did you say?"

"Oh yeah, and the sisters are selling herbal tea online as a fund-raiser," Ella says.

"Tea?" Ben is completely lost now.

Ella and I look at each other and say at the same time, "Sanctity Tea. 'It's not only for relaxing, it's for giving.'"

"Get it?" Ella asks.

"For-giving!" I add.

"Stop!" Ben says. "Overload. Tell it to me in chro–no–log–i–cal order."

By the time we reach Gusty's, Ella and I have given Ben a blow-by-blow of our adventures. Before we walk into the parking lot, I slap myself in the forehead. "That's why they have the lights on all night. They're *grow* lights. They're growing plants for tea in the solarium."

"People must *really* like this tea," Ben says. "And that explains the fifty-pound bags of bat guano."

"Whose car is that?" Ella asks. She's pointing to the black Escalade.

"Oh, no," Ben groans. "They're back."

"The rockers," I say.

I feel her hand on my arm. "Rock stars? Which rock stars?"

"Rock-*ers*, not *stars*."

Ben laughs.

"What are their names?" she asks.

"We don't know," Ben says. "They're tattooed

and wear rock band clothes. That's all. I don't think they're even musicians."

"I call the big guy Skullfinger," I say, "because he wears a skull ring."

"What are they doing here?" she asks.

"Being obnoxious," I say. "You'll see. They love the lobster fries."

Ella shivers. "Lobster on fries. Yuck. I'll just take the fries, please."

"It's not lobster on fries. It's fries you eat with lobster. Extra-crunchy with a bowl of melted butter with saffron and lime juice for dipping." Ben sounds like Dad explaining the menu to summer people. "They're really good."

"Whatevs," she says. "Let's go see these pseudo rock stars."

28

My eyeballs bug out when we walk in Gusty's and I see Mom sitting at a table with the rockers, showing them pictures of property for sale in Maiden Rock. Dad bangs around behind the counter, drying his hands and shooting negative vibes toward Mom's real-estate presentation.

Ella, Ben and I flop down at our table, and Dad brings over bottles of Moxie, glasses of ice, and a bowl of Cheese Nips.

"*Them?*" I whisper.

Dad has his back to her and peeks over his shoulder before he shakes his head ever so slightly. "Go figure."

Ella cranes her neck to see around Dad. "Who are they? Are they in a band?"

"I guess you guys would have to tell me that. I don't know much about bands these days."

Dad is right about that. When I asked him last year what song he wanted as a ring tone, he said "Jumpin' Jack Flash" by the Rolling Stones. Like it was totally cool and I would be impressed. Then he said, "What? The Rolling Stones are one of the most influential bands in the history of rock music." Groan. At least he didn't claim that the Rolling Stones were the uncontested kings of rock 'n' roll.

Skullfinger looks at each page Mom gives him and shakes his head. Mom tries a few more. No. No. No. Then Skullfinger gestures out the window, toward the point, and says a lot of stuff like "that way" and "you're not hearing me." Finally, he sits back in his chair and tosses the pages on the table. The over-head light reflects off the gold cross dangling from his ear. His tone is demanding—like Mom should find him what he wants or he'll talk to another real estate agent. She sits patiently and gives him her full attention.

The earring is a tiny version of the cross the other guy, Stevie, wears around his neck. I pop the top on my Moxie and pour it over the ice. Fizz travels like a cloud over my hand.

"What are we drinking?" Ella looks in my glass.

"Moxie," Ben and I say at the same time.

Ben launches into everything-you-ever-wanted-to-know mode. "It's the oldest soda in the United States. It's from 1884. It's, like, even older than ginger ale."

Ella snaps her tab and pours the sparkly soda. She watches it like it might be poison, then lifts the glass to her lips and takes the teeniest sip.

"Ugh! It tastes like toothpaste," she says. "I'll take a coffee."

Dad, Ben, and I laugh.

"Let me bring you guys some Gusty burgers and lobster fries," Dad says.

"I'll take a burger but no lobster fries for me," Ella wrinkles her nose.

Clearly, she wasn't paying attention when Ben explained what they were.

Dad walks away wearily. He is not enjoying the afternoon.

As we wait, I catch more snippets of the conversation between Skullfinger and Mom: ". . . That old joint . . . Premium oceanfront." I begin to get it: he's interested in the convent, and Mom's trying to explain that it isn't on the market. But she isn't discouraging him either. She says things like, "I'll contact the archdiocese and tell them there is an interested buyer." Skullfinger likes this. Then I hear Mom say, "If it's okay with the monsignor, I'll get an appraiser out to determine a current value." Skullfinger wants to "get in and take a look." Mom tries to put him off a "day or so."

As the rockers pull the café door closed behind them, Skullfinger draws a pack of cigarettes out of his pocket and pulls one out with his lips. Mom calls out, "I'll get back to you as soon as I hear. Tomorrow morning. Yes, I'm sure, tomorrow morning."

I can tell she's in real-estate dream state as she walks to our table.

"What are you doing, Mom?"

"I'm trying to improve Maiden Rock, that's what I'm doing. They want to develop the property into condos."

"Those guys?" Ben's eyebrows arch.

"I knew they were real rock stars," Ella says.

"Who are they?" I ask.

Mom pulls a paper out of her stack and reads, "John Bard."

"I never heard of any musician named John Bard," Ben says.

"Who said they were rock stars?" Mom asks.

Dad arrives with the food and jumps into the conversation. "If those guys aren't rock stars, where will they get the money to buy the convent and develop condos?"

"What? I can't believe you're judging them by their appearance," Mom says.

Instead of joining the argument, I think *cigarettes, necklace, earrings.* What if these guys were the ones smoking cigarettes behind the Abbots? What if they weren't lost and looking for Rook River? What if they were casing the empty houses along the coast? What if they're not innocent real estate buyers or even buyers at all? What if they just want to get in the convent and see if there's anything to steal, like Virgin Mary statues or golden chalices?

Now my brain is on fire. What if they have something to do with Ms. Stillford's being gone? And *why isn't Mom thinking the same thing?* That was her theory—burglars!

"Do they know you're the sheriff?" I ask.

"They called my Maiden Rock Realty line," Mom says. "I had no reason to mention it."

"What about Ms. Stillford? Aren't you going to search tomorrow?" I look at her like, *I can't believe you're not putting this together!*

She calls me over to the other side of the room.

"I took her lobster brooch to the jeweler in Rook River and had it appraised," Mom whispers. "It's worth twelve thousand dollars." She looks at me like, *Are you going to tell me this isn't a robbery motive?*

I'm about to say the rockers may be the ones with the robbery motive when she cuts me off. "So I'm going to turn the investigation over to the Rook River Police and the state police and the FBI. They have the resources to expand the search beyond Maiden Rock."

I don't believe this. Can't she see what's right in front of her? Is she that focused on a possible real estate deal?

I look over at the table where Ben is showing Ella how to eat a lobster fry and she's laughing at him.

"Saffron," Ben says. "Don't they have saffron in New York City?" Ella responds by picking up a fry, making an exaggerated swish around the butter cup, and arcing it to her mouth. I check the window to see if the rockers' Escalade is gone.

Mom's eyes follow mine.

"What, Quinn? What is it?"

I want to say something about the rockers being suspects, but I'm pretty sure that will get me another big lecture about staying out of the investigation. I calculate that she won't be too surprised or upset if I casually ask about my original suspect. "Mom, did you interview Owen Loney?"

"Yes. Yes, I did."

"And?"

"And he's worried sick about Blythe. The man's a wreck. He wants me to ride on his boat up and down the coast with him looking for her. He wants me to call the FBI, the CIA, the NSA, and *CSI*. If he's the one who kidnapped her, that's pretty bizarre behavior."

Now I'm sure that telling her about the bloody hook and the T-shirt would be useless. She's made up her mind about him. And all of a sudden, I'm maybe changing mine a little too. That could have been dried ketchup.

"Okay. I gotta go eat." I turn away from her. I need to start investigating whether the rockers are robbers. I need to find proof. That's what convinces sheriffs. Proof.

I feel Mom's hand on my shoulder. "Quinnie?"

I wait.

"I love you, Quinn. I know you love Blythe. We will find her. They will find her. They have the resources to find her. And I'm not giving up. I'm just broadening the search."

I walk to my table and plop down, but I can't eat a single lobster fry.

Ella, however, can't stop eating them. Of course— first timers never can. But she finally gets to the Gusty burger and oohs and aahs her way through that.

"You could totally make a zillion dollars with these in the city. People would go Whac-A-Mole over them."

"I need to go home," I say.

Ella looks at me with a sad face like she doesn't want to leave the plate of lobster fries or Ben.

I push back my chair, but not before Owen Loney bursts through the door and marches straight in our direction.

29

"This yours, girl?" Owen Loney says. He slides my phone across the table. Ella almost chokes on a fry.

Dad quickly walks over. "Hi, Owen, what's up?"

Owen Loney's face is as red as a boiled lobster. "Found that phone."

Dad looks at it, then at me. "Quinnie? Is that yours?

No use denying it. "Yes. I lost it."

"On my boat," Owen Loney says. "Where she had no business being."

I go for the closest to the truth. "I was showing Ella a lobster boat."

As soon as I say it, I realize how stupid it sounds. It's not close enough.

Owen Loney snorts.

"Okay, let's simmer down here," Dad says.

"I'll simmer down when she brings back what she took," Owen Loney says.

"Quinnie? Did you take something from the *Blythe Spirit*?" Dad says.

I can't believe it. He's not saying "Give me back my hook," but I know what he wants. I turn to Ella for support. She's slunk down in her chair.

"She better bring it back," Owen Loney barks.

Give him back the incriminating evidence? No way. I completely forget that a minute ago I was considering the rockers as suspects. "Maybe Mr. Loney can explain why he was mentioned in Ms. Stillford's letter?" I add a silent *humph* with my chin.

"She was trying to send me a message," he yells. "To save her!" Droplets of spit fly out of his mouth and land near the platter of lobster fries.

"Or she was trying to tell Mom that you—"

"Okay! Okay! Okay!" Dad steps in between our table and Owen Loney, putting his hand against Owen Loney's chest and turning him around. As Owen Loney moves toward the door, he yells, "Fool girl!"

"Just a kid," Dad says as they go outside, ". . . loves Blythe . . . we're all worried sick . . ."

"Did you hear that?" I shout at Ella and Ben. My heart is pounding in my ears. "He thinks her letter is a message to *him*! That's ridiculous." I'm not sure why I'm so worked up. A few minutes ago, I was thinking of scratching him off the suspect list.

Ben and Ella are looking at me with eyes the size of pie plates.

Dad returns, shaking his head. "Quinnie—"

"Don't say anything."

"I'm not saying anything other than everybody's upset about Blythe, but we can't take it out on each other."

"You don't know—"

"You're right," Dad says. "I don't know everything that's going on, but I know this. You need to calm down. And you need to return whatever you took from Owen's boat first thing tomorrow." His right cheek is twitching, which I have only seen once before. (It involved a broken refrigerator and three days' worth of spoiled crabmeat.) He takes a breath and says, "You and Mariella should head home now. You too, Ben."

Ella opens her mouth to say something, but Ben interrupts her. "She prefers Ella, like Ella Marvell."

Ella snaps, "I *think* I can tell him that *myself*."

"Fine, fine. Everybody's a little on edge. You girls get going," Dad says. Ben shrinks like a deflated balloon, gets up, zips his hoodie with a jerk, and leaves. Through the window, I see him take off running toward home.

Before Ella and I are even out the door, Dad pulls

out his phone. He's calling Mom, for sure. What a mess.

On the walk home, I can't stop repeating every word Owen Loney said and every word I said.

"That was crazy," Ella says. "I couldn't believe how you pounced on old Owen Loney. He was spitting mad."

"My mom won't be as impressed as you are."

"So stay over at my house tonight."

* * *

Mr. Philpotts smiles when Ella tells him I'm staying over.

"Good. I'm being interviewed by the publisher of the *Rook River Valley Advertiser* over dinner in Rook River," he says. "You girls can figure out something to eat, right?"

"We just ate," Ella says. "Gusty burgers and lobster fries."

"That's sounds pretty down east, *ayuh*?" he says and laughs at himself. "Hey, do I sound like a Mainiac?"

I almost hate to smack him down, but I do it for his own good. "*Mainahs*, not Mainiacs. And only really old guys who wear L.L.Bean hats with earflaps are allowed to say *ayuh*."

He considers this for a second, then says, "Thanks for the tip."

"I figured you didn't want to sound like the summer people or anything."

When I call Mom to ask her if I can stay over at Ella's, she says, "Fine," and I can tell from the tone of her "fine" that she's heard about the Owen Loney incident from Dad and she's trying to keep a lid on her temper.

* * *

When Mr. Philpotts is gone, Ella leads me into her dad's study.

"I wonder what Ben's doing," I say. "He looked kind of bummed."

"That guy needs a time out. Really."

I shrug my shoulders like *maybe*, but I really mean *maybe not*.

"What?" Ella says. "Do you like him?"

I grab a magazine and flip through the pages. I didn't expect a writer's study to have stacks of bird magazines: *Bird Watching*, *Bird Talk*, *Living Bird*, and five pairs of binoculars. "Is your dad a bird-watcher?"

"No. He's writing a murder mystery about three women where one of them kills the others over who sees the most birds in a year. When he researches a novel he really gets into it. But you're trying to change the subject." Ella pulls the magazine from my hands and looks me eye to eye. "Tell the truth. I mean, you know, do you *like*-like Ben?"

I think I am going to say "yes," but instead what pops out is, "I've known him all my life."

She turns back to the bookshelf. "There is an endless supply of cute guys in New York, you know. You could come and visit me after we go back, if you want."

She sounds like Zoe. She thinks I only like Ben because he's the only boy in town all year round. And maybe I should meet the guys in New York, but I don't want to. I'm loyal to Ben. Of course, Ben doesn't know this.

Ella pulls some books off the shelf and flops onto the leather sofa. "I'm not saying he's not cute—in a *Mainah* kind of way—it's just that there are soooo many guys in the world who don't answer your questions for you."

"He wasn't being rude," I say. And I wonder why I'm defending him to her. I'd be better off if she thought he was a creep. But he wasn't being rude. He was being Ben, Mr. Walking Wikipedia.

"Look at this." Ella hands me a mystery novel.

The cover has dark shadows, sharp angles, and the chalk outline of a body. *The Hard-Boiled Boneyard.*

"What's it about?"

"It's about a man who loves a woman, but she won't love him back, so he bonks her on the head."

I get chills.

"And this." Ella hands me *The Homely Heart.* It has a torn valentine on the cover.

"What's this about?"

"He pushes her off a bridge."

"Does your dad let you read these?

"Are you kidding? No way. But I do anyway." She climbs on a stool and reaches for another one. "And this. *Dark Observer.* He hangs around the investigation and he offers to help. He's really nice to her family, but all the time he has her locked in his basement."

"Yuck. Don't show me any more."

An old-fashioned clock on the shelf is ticking loud enough to echo in my head. Ella is reaching for another book when I stop her.

"Wait. Listen. It might not be Owen Loney."

"What? Owen Loney totally did it," she says. "If there's a basement in that lobster pound, your teacher is in it."

"There's no basement in the pound. And besides,

he wants to take Mom searching up and down the coast with his boat and call the FBI." I pause to get her full attention. "I think maybe it's those rockers. I think they're robbers."

"The rockers are robbers? And they kidnapped Ms. Stillford? Are you kidding? Have you lost your little Maine mind?"

"Listen. Suppose the rockers knew Ms. Stillford had valuable jewelry, like her ruby lobster pin. And suppose they went to her house to steal it, and somehow she discovered them, and they kidnapped her to keep her quiet." I feel a little like Mom with my *supposes.*

"If they kidnapped her, why are they trying to buy property in Maiden Rock?

"Maybe they don't want to buy property. That's an excuse to get into the convent and see what there is to steal."

"Yeah, but if they did something to Ms. Stillford, why aren't they miles and miles from the scene of the crime?" She gathers the books and puts them back on the shelf in the exact right places. "And what about the bloody hook and the T-shirt?" Ella says.

"It could have been a big fish that tried to jump in the boat, and he had to kill it."

Now I'm defending Owen Loney.

30

I stop in the doorway of Ella's room. I almost can't remember when it was perfectly Zoe. The papier-mâché moose head, the hundreds of black-and-white beach photos, the ukulele—all gone. In such a short time it has become so perfectly Ella: sparkles, crazy shoes, makeup, Ella Marvell posters. Zoe's room is getting a new life while Ms. Stillford could be losing hers.

My eyes rest on a book on the bed with a teen girl on the cover. She's wearing dark clothes and a backpack and crawling out of a window. The title of the book is *I Love You, He Lied*.

If the kidnapper is not John Denby or Owen Loney, I think, then he didn't do it for love. And Ms. Stillford is probably in really, really serious danger. I concentrate on all the puzzle pieces and come up with new pictures.

Ella is at her desk, applying purple eye shadow in the mirror. She continues as she talks. "Okay. Let me get this straight. If the rockers are robbers, they're casing the convent for . . . what? Jewel-encrusted Virgin Marys?"

I look at her in the mirror and think about this and say, "Yes. They're off-season beach-house burglars."

"And that Escalade is full of what? Stolen beach towels and plastic wine glasses?" She raises her left eyebrow and looks at me. "Those cute little grabbers for a hot ear of corn?"

I flop on her bed and consider this logic. "Okay, well, maybe that's not it. But why else would they want to look inside the convent?"

"Maybe they're cat burglars and they've come for the cats. Hallelujah!"

Okay, that was a little funny.

I roll a piece of bedspread lint into a ball and prepare to flick it on the floor when Ella says, "Hey, don't do that."

Yikes. I look around. The room doesn't look so clean that it can't take a lint ball on the floor.

"Put it here." Ella hands me a jar full of colorful threads of cotton and wool.

"What do you do with it?"

"I twist it together into a thread and sew it into

a hoodie." She fishes three wads of lint out of the jar and begins to shred and reshape them with her fingertips, rolling and pulling until a single thin thread of red, gold, and green forms. "See?" She loops it around her finger, then stuffs the loop in her pocket. Then she tosses me a blue hoodie that has been hanging on the back of her chair. There's an S-curve of blended color stitched inside the edge of the hood.

"Cool," I say.

"I'll do it to yours, if you want."

"Sure. Thanks."

"Just save your lint." I can't explain it, but this makes my eyes well up. Ella turns away and says, "Hey, tell me more about those beach-house burglars."

I take a deep breath to refocus on the rockers. "The cigarette butts at Horror House may have been theirs."

"Maybe, but who cares if they're smoking behind an old house?"

"Ben said the sisters' van was parked at the Abbotts a while ago. Maybe—"

Ella finishes my sentence: "—they're following the sisters around, stalking them for their rosaries." From her tone, I wonder if she's making fun of me, but she's stretching her eyelid and applying glitter at the same time, so I'm not sure.

"Both those guys *were* wearing crosses." I laugh at my own joke. "But the sisters were probably just back there picking herbs for their tea."

"Wait, wait, I know—the rockers are in search of a for-giving tea."

"If there's a lot of it, it could be worth something, right?"

The thought makes me want to know exactly what the rockers are looking for. But mostly, I want to talk to Ben. I want to know he's okay after the slap down he got from Ella.

I tell Ella that I'm going to text him, and she says, "Why? It's late."

But I do it anyway: *Come to Ella's up the beach way*

He takes five minutes to reply: *Why?*

Just as I thought, he's pouting. *To go with us to investigate the convent*

He replies: *Why?*

I want to text him, *don't be a dope,* but instead I type: *They may want valuable stuff in there*

He replies: *What are you talking about?*

This time I text it: *Chalices, statues*

Then I realize he's way behind on the state of our investigation. I stop texting and call him.

"Hey. Look, those rockers may have been breaking into houses and walked in on Ms. Stillford and had to kidnap her and hide her away. Now I think they're sniffing around the convent for valuables. We want to investigate it. Will you come?"

He hesitates long enough for me to know that he's still a little wounded. "Sure."

"Oh, and can you pick some of those leaves on the trampled path behind Horror House?"

"Leaves behind—"

"Just some of the leaves—from the bushes—on the path, you know."

"Oh-*kay*."

"Meet us on the beach by Ella's."

Saying *Ella's*, not *Zoe's*, makes me feel a pinch disloyal. I look up to see Ella is rummaging in the bottom of her closet. She looks like she's been here for a year. When I get another text, I assume it's Ben trying to weasel out of going with us, but it's not from him at all. It's from the mystery texter: *Following the little things can send you in circles. Ignoring them can stop you flat.*

"Well, that's the truth," I mumble to myself.

"What?" Ella says in a muffled voice from the closet.

"What are you doing in your closet?"

"What?"

I walk to the closet and lean over. "Look at this," I say.

Ella stands up and backs out, pushing me out of

the way. "Sheesh, just getting a hoodie. I don't think we're both going to fit in there."

I hold my phone in her face. "I couldn't agree more," she says.

But I'm sure I've caught her this time. "Do you have your phone in the closet?"

"My phone is water-dead. You know that."

"Let me see."

She walks to her desk and the hands her phone to me. The screen is black as coal. I press every button and tap the surface. Dead. Dead. Dead.

"Satisfied?" Ella says.

"I want to look in your closet."

"Be my guest."

I crawl around the bottom of her closet and notice even more strange shoes but no other phone. So maybe she isn't sending the texts.

"If I had another phone, the text ID would be different," Ella says. She flops on her bed with her hand out. "Give me your phone again."

Together we look at each of the text messages.

"They all have one thing in common," Ella says. "They're brilliant."

Then I do the one thing I keep forgetting to do. I check my photos. It's still there—the picture I took of Owen Loney's T-shirt. He had a chance to delete it and he didn't. Not only did he give the phone back, he didn't poke around in it like a real kidnapper might have.

* * *

The gusts coming off the ocean make me wish I'd worn the hoodie that Ella offered me. Maybe the colored thread would've worked as a charm against the cold wind. Ella has wrapped a scarf over the fleece that she pulled over a sweater that's covering a T-shirt.

"I will never let myself get as cold and wet as I was by that stupid lobster boat," she says. "I think I'm coming down with something."

One of her dad's many bird binoculars is hanging around her neck. She couldn't find gloves so she's pulled her sleeves down and wrapped them around her hands. We are kicking cold wet sand in the dark and waiting for Ben.

I can't stop thinking about the text messages. The advice isn't "brilliant" like Ella says. It isn't even all that useful. But someone is sending them to help me find Ms. Stillford, and I'm finally convinced they aren't from Ella.

As Ella and I hop around to stay warm, I try to think of all the people it might be. Mom. No. Dad.

No. Ben. Maybe. But probably not. Owen Loney. Heck no. Even on a cloudy night, I can still see the lines of whitecaps pounding at the shore. The surf seems noisier in the dark. I can barely hear Ella complaining about the smell of dead seaweed and the stench of stranded crabs.

A shadowy figure appears at the south end of the beach. It's jogging toward us.

Ella raises the binoculars. "It's him."

As Ben gets closer, he waves a plastic bag above his head. "I hope I got what you wanted," he yells.

I grab the bag and pull out some leaves, trying to remember if they look like the plants in the potting shed and the botany books.

"Here, I'll put it inside." Ella grabs the bag and starts running to her porch. "I can't stand it. I'm going to look for my gloves again."

While she's gone, I lean in toward Ben and ask, "You okay?"

He looks up the dune toward her house and says, "She's, like, *really* from New York."

I look in the same direction. "Yeah, she is."

He doesn't look like he wants to talk about it anymore, and I'm fine with that, so I count waves breaking at our feet. *Three, four, five . . . eleven, twelve*, and Ella runs back up to us and claps her hands, which are now covered with huge mittens. "My dad's," she says. "Okay, Mainahs, let's go do this thing."

We start jogging toward the convent, and Ben asks me, "What's this thing we're doing again?"

"We're checking for valuable Virgin Marys, silver stuff, gold stuff, anything that the rockers might want. If those sleazeballs are connected to Ms. Stillford's disappearance," I tell him, "we're going to get one step ahead of them. Maybe they'll lead us to where they're hiding Ms. Stillford."

We splash through ankle-deep pools of icy seawater and slip on rubbery Irish moss. Ella's pants are tucked into her sparkle high-tops so her legs are somewhat protected from the cold. I'm wearing boat shoes without socks, and the foam stings my ankles. Ben's got on jeans, socks, and old running shoes. Even if he's knee-deep in frigid surf, he'll never admit he's uncomfortable. But we can't stay out here too long.

Soon the convent looms before us on the crest above the rocky beach.

Ella stares up at Our Lady of the Tides and shakes her head. Strands of her hair lash her face. "Not going up there," she says.

I shudder when I look at the place. A whistling sound pierces the thrashing of the ocean. It takes a second to register.

The cry of cats.

A chorus of cats is perched on the rocks above us, watching and hissing out warnings to stay away. I can't see individual felines, only sets of yellow eyes.

"Now that's cool," Ben says. He snaps a picture with his phone. The flash goes off. I slap him hard on the back of his head.

"What?" he says.

"We are *sneaking* here. *Sneaking!*"

The faint sound of a motorboat catches my ear. I spin around and spy a small craft approaching from the south. It has no running lights, but it's coming fast. Its hull slams the ocean surface and throws up a wide wake.

Ben points to a pile of boulders at the water's edge. I beckon Ella to follow us, and together we crawl sideways like crabs across the smaller rocks and through puddles of standing water. As the boat bounces its way toward the shore, the three of us slip between two rocks, pressing our fingertips into the crevices.

The motor glub–glubs as the boat bobs and lurches and rolls. If the craft comes any closer, if it crosses the breakers it risks scuttling on the rocks. To be safe, it will have to beach closer to the open shoreline or moor in deeper water.

After about a minute, the motor dies.

"Who it is?" I ask Ben.

"Two guys. That's all I can see," he says.

In front of me, Ella is trying to focus the binoculars using the thumbs of her oversized mittens.

"Is it Skullfinger?" I ask her.

She shrugs her shoulders—she can't tell. I swipe my thumb across one of the lenses.

"Not helping," she says and wipes the lens on her sleeve like I smeared it.

The figures are dark. Dark jackets with dark hoods. Wisps of their conversation blow ashore.

"Yo . . . man . . . anchor"

". . . can't . . . find . . ."

". . . free . . . zing . . ."

I feel something vibrating near my shoulder and turn to see Ben's phone moving in his pocket. He yanks it out. *Uncle John* shows up on the screen. Ella slaps her mitten over the phone to cover the glow of the display and sends it flying from Ben's hands into the tangle of seaweed behind us. "Hey!" Ben snaps.

"Stevie! Get in . . . water," one of the men in the boat yells at the other.

"Ain't no way," Stevie yells back.

No doubt about it now. It's Skullfinger and his buddy.

"See, I told you!" I whisper.

"A couple of idiots," Ben says. "They can't figure out how to get out of the boat."

"Even if they get to shore, I don't see how they think they're going to be able to get away with any stolen stuff," I say.

We watch them struggle until they give up, restart the motor, and head back down the coast. Ella sniffles in my ear the whole time.

"Now I've got to find my probably-smashed phone," Ben says. He doesn't look at Ella. I can tell he's mad.

We crawl over the wet, slippery rocks, looking for Ben's phone with no success.

"Quinnie, call Ben's phone with your phone," Ella says. "Maybe it will light up."

I do, and it does. Ben scrambles over to the phone and fishes it out of a knot of seaweed.

He's wiping sand off the screen when he says to Ella, "That was a good idea."

"Sorry I wacked it," she says and wipes her nose with her big woolly paw.

"Sorry I butted in about your name. At Gusty's." She shrugs.

He holds out his hand to help her across the rocks.

31

Ella takes Ben's hand and—*groan*—doesn't let go right away. And just like that, they're friends again, and it's them and me. I hear Ms. Stillford say, "Name the feelings, Quinn." And the only words that come to mind are *heart pain*.

"Hey, you're shaking all over," Ben says to Ella.

"Big surprise. It's freezing out here." Ella sneezes. "I feel feverish."

Ben gives me a pressing look. "I'm thinking maybe we should go back."

At that exact moment, the lights snap on from the top of the convent and flood the beach.

"Those guys may be coming back any minute," Ella says.

"I don't think so," I say. "Not with all this light. Plus, I don't think they can manage the boat." I glance up at the solarium windows. If one of the sisters looks out now, we'll be center stage. "Come on, let's get out of here. I don't think anybody will be sneaking in the convent tonight."

Down the coast, there's not a boat in sight, just whitecap after whitecap. "They'll come by land tomorrow. They'll get Mom to take them right to the house. That's where we need to be."

* * *

When we get back to the Philpotts', I fix Ella a mug of boiling water with a couple of cough drops plunked in it. That's the best I can do. She leans her face over it and breathes in deeply. Then I tell her and Ben what we're going to do.

"Tomorrow morning, before Mom and the rockers show up, Ella and I are going to sneak into the convent and poke around."

"Can you wait until I get back from school?"

"Sorry. We have to get there before Mom and the rockers."

"I'm going to need three more of these cough-drop drinks if I'm going on a break-in that early," Ella says.

The bag that Ben brought from the marsh is on the table in front of us. I grab it and pull out a few leaves. "Maybe I can make you some relaxing tea."

The leaves look like what I saw on the seed packets in Ms. Stillford's shed. Shiny with pointy tips. I bruise them and start to sniff. *Phew*—I throw them back in the bag. "You better stick to the cough-drop brew."

*   *   *

I toss and turn in my sleep, refining the plan and continuing to guess who might be sending me texts. John Denby. No. Zoe. No. Officer Dobson. Ha, ha—no.

At six the next morning, Ella's dad is snoring so loudly he wakes us up. We're dressed and packing for our reconnaissance when I get a text message from Mom: *Q--Taking clients to convent but see you at cafe for lunch. Hey how do you make a heart on these things?*

I show it to Ella. "Bingo."

"Aren't you going to tell your mom about the rockers being on the beach last night?"

I imagine how the conversation would go. I'd tell her that her big real estate clients may have kidnapped Ms. Stillford. She'd look at me like she brought the wrong baby home from the hospital. Then she'd act calm and ask me why I think that. And I'd be forced to tell her that it's a hunch.

Oh, and if I told her about Skullfinger and Stevie on the boat last night, she'd have plenty of questions for me, like what I was doing out there, and would I swear in court that it positively was the rockers. And I'd have to say I couldn't absolutely swear it in court because it was dark, but I'm pretty sure, and basically, Mom would ground me for life, and I would never be allowed to go anywhere ever again, not even to college . . .

"No," I say and resume packing. "I'm not going to tell her."

"What if something goes wrong?"

"My mom's the sheriff. She'll be right there—with them most of the day."

"What if they kidnap your mom?"

"Now that would be *really* dumb."

"Monroe Spalding says, 'If they were Einsteins, they wouldn't be gangsters.'"

I roll my eyes. "Keep packing."

⁂

We go over my checklist: black pants, black T-shirts, black hoodies—Ella's has a silver sequin heart on the front, so I make her turn it inside out—dark shoes, black binoculars.

"Why exactly are we going *noir*?" Ella asks. "It's daytime."

"It's dim in the convent," I reply. "I'm thinking black is better than sparkle. Doesn't Monroe Spalding go low profile in dark spaces?"

"Sounds good," she says, and she sounds good too. Not even a sneeze or sniffle this morning, although I'm feeling a little warm.

When we're ready, I call Dad at the café.

"Hi, honey. You and Ella have a good night?"

"It was okay."

"You're gonna give Owen back whatever it was you took from the boat? This morning? First thing? Right?"

Whoa. I haven't thought about the gaff hook or Owen Loney since yesterday. It seems like it all happened a month ago. There is no way we have time to dig it up this morning.

"Yes, Dad. I'll take it back as soon as I can."

"You girls get something to eat?"

"Plenty. Ella's house has food too, you know."

Ella's giving me a wrap-it-up signal.

"Well, come to the café any time you're hungry," Dad says. "And Quinnie, it's pretty cold outside today. Bundle up. Love you."

"I will, Dad. Love you, Dad."

I turn to Ella. "Ready?"

"Are we taking the gaff hook back to the Pound?"

"Nope. Not now. We've got more important things to do."

"Do you think we should text Ben and tell him we're on our way?"

"Sure," I say, but I don't make a move to take out my phone.

"So, can I use your phone? Mine is drowned, remember."

I hand it over, and Ella's hands go to work.

Watching her text Ben pains me, but I shake it off. What matters now is Ms. Stillford.

"One more thing," Ella says. "You need some eye shadow. So what's it going to be? *Sri Lankan Sapphire Blue* or *Garden of Midnight Temptations Green*?"

32

My eyelids feel a little heavy with the *Sri Lankan Sapphire Blue* plastered from corner to corner. Ella's shimmer with *Garden of Midnight Temptations Green*. She says eye shadow lifts and brightens our eyes, but it feels more like a mask, which might be okay if it makes us invisible.

We sneak up the beach, past the scene of Skullfinger and Stevie's botched boat landing last night. We climb the rocks up to the dense tree line and cut back through the woods until we're hidden in the bushes across from the convent front door.

My phone vibrates in my pocket. It's a text from Ben. Ella and I huddle close to read it at the same time.

Don't get into trouble before I get home

"Aww," Ella says. "That's sweet."

I study her face to see if she's being sarcastic. She's not.

"Come on, let's go, Monroe Spalding."

* * *

An hour later, Ella and I are still crouched in the bushes waiting for something to happen. The seats of our pants are damp from the cold morning dew. When I touch my face, I can feel the heat radiating off of it. I pull away my scarf to cool my neck. Ella has her hands clamped over her nose and mouth. Cats have been picking their way through the leaves to greet us.

"Go away, kitties!" I whisper.

Ella swats at them, which only attracts more. Some of them are purring. Spiro is among them.

The convent van is parked in the circular driveway. I look at my phone. *9:17 a.m.*

I'm about to tell Ella to hand me the binoculars when the convent's front door opens. Sister Rosie steps out with a white apron around her waist, lugging two huge bowls. The cats yowl and bolt toward her. We scrunch low. She talks to them in a soft, musical voice.

"Good morning, lovelies. Are you hungry?" She looks around as cats come leaping toward her from every direction. "Hello, Rocky. Hello, Bell . . . Wait a minute, who's missing?"

Ella whispers in my ear: "How could she ever know who's missing?"

I'm about to say I have no idea when a white cat with orange spots lumbers down the driveway and joins the breakfast crowd.

"Esmeralda! There you are." Sister Rosie bends over and puts the bowls down. "Here you go. Tuna and kibble and peas and carrots."

She stands up, presses her hands to her lower back, and looks to the sky while she groans through a stretch. I freeze as she begins to scan the trees nearby. Her eyes appear to fix on us, but they keep moving. She sighs and says, "Another crisp autumn day."

No sooner has Sister Rosie closed the big front door than Mom's real estate SUV pulls up in front of the convent, followed by a red sedan. Some of the cats scatter; others keep eating. A woman in a black raincoat, clutching a clipboard and a pen, gets out of the red car.

The woman looks at the convent like it's a piece of art in a museum, then wrinkles her nose and scratches notes on her clipboard.

Mom holds her hand up in front of the woman. "Let me talk to them first."

Mom barely gets that out before the door opens and Sister Ethel steps outside. The sister's pointy expression makes her look thinner and bonier than usual.

"Sister." Mom clears her throat. "I assume you got a call from the monsignor this morning?"

"We did." It's not a friendly reply.

Mom moves toward the door like she expects Sister Ethel to step aside, but Sister Ethel blocks the way with her body. Mom's posture subtly shifts from real estate agent to sheriff. I get a prickly feeling on the back of my neck.

Mom reaches into her real estate lady briefcase, snaps out a piece of paper, and hands it to Sister Ethel. The woman with the clipboard steps forward and sticks out her hand. "How do you do, Sister? I'm Laura Burnside, the appraiser. All I really need to do is take a quick walk-through and ask a few questions. I can get most of what I need from the public records. It won't take long . . . really."

Sister Ethel's arm drops to her side, and the paper flutters to the ground. Mom leans over and picks it up. Sister Rosie appears in the doorway and hands paper cups to Mom and the appraiser.

"Some nice cocoa for a cool Maine morning," Sister Rosie says.

Sister Ethel tells the appraiser, "The monsignor says you can look around on the main floor and that's all. This is both a home and a place of prayer. No going upstairs to private quarters or into the chapel. Those are the rules." She juts her chin like these rules are non-negotiable.

Mom steps backward and looks up at the convent roof. The appraiser's eyes follow her. The sisters don't move.

"I think that will be fine," Mom says. "What do you think, Laura?"

"I suppose I can extrapolate from the first floor," Laura says.

"Good, then. Let's get this over with," Mom says.

The sisters back up into the convent, clearing the way for Mom and the appraiser.

I turn to Ella, and I grab my backpack. "Let's go!"

We leap up and bolt across the driveway. Just before the big door closes completely, I grab the handle to stop it. Ella rushes up behind me. We wait for the voices inside to grow faint then we quietly slip into the dark foyer.

33

A musty smell engulfs us, and thick dust particles find their way up my nose. I muffle a cough in my armpit. It takes me a second to adjust my eyes and to remember what's what.

I haven't been in the convent for almost five years, when the nuns hosted a Christmas Open House. In those days, more sisters lived here—maybe ten, and they showed us all around: up the front staircase and down the hallway. A brass number was the only identification on each of the sister's bedroom doors, one through ten. At the end, the two French doors opened up into a stupendous solarium that smelled of balsam and sticky pine. From the solarium, we went down the back stairway to the kitchen for hot apple cider and ginger cookies.

The space is the same, but the mood is drearier. Ella and I crouch behind the big, fat spindle at the base of the staircase and look into the large living room. Worn chairs crowd around small tables holding lamps with frayed, yellowed shades. An old upright piano with no bench stands against the wall. The seat cushion of a stuffed leather chair is split open, and stuffing puffs out like an exploded popcorn kernel. The place does not look like it's home to gold crosses or jeweled rosaries.

The room after the living room is the dining hall, where the sisters, Mom, and the appraiser stand by a long rectangular table, like they're in a scene from some old painting.

I tap Ella on the shoulder and wave for her to follow me up the massive carved staircase. We hunch over and take each step slowly until my foot presses on a creaky board.

The adults stop talking. We curl up like snails, hoping the large spindles will hide us.

"What was that?" Mom says.

"Oh, this old building has arthritis," says Sister Rosie. "The aches and pains of old age."

A conversation about the condition of the roof starts up, and no one looks our way. I motion to Ella, and we head up the steps.

The convent gets warmer as we reach the second floor landing. Brighter, too. The bedroom doors are all closed. At the end, I spot a large room, dense with greenery. "That's the solarium," I whisper to Ella.

Downstairs, Mom shouts, "Sisters? We're leaving now. I'll be back with our interested party in a few minutes."

I listen for the sisters' response but can't hear them. I feel exposed in the middle of the hallway. Ella and I look at each other, and without saying a word, we take off running for the solarium.

No sooner do we cross the threshold than we hear the sisters' rising voices through the sea of leaves. They must have come up the back stairway. Ella and I drop to the floor and crawl on our bellies into the middle of the room until we're under one of the wooden tables that support the plants. Through sagging loops of plastic tubing and wiring for grow-lights, I can see the sisters' black skirts coming toward us.

They're arguing.

"Hurry, Rosie. Pick the tea," Sister Ethel says.

"Even if it's not ready?" asks Sister Rosie.

"Pick it. Pick it all right now and bag it. I just got another email."

"What did they say this time?" asks Sister Rosie.

The skirts move closer to us, and we tuck in our arms and legs as tightly as possible.

"Let's get rid of it all. We'll give them their last

big order and be done with it. Be done with them," Sister Ethel says. "We're not cut out to be farmers."

"We were fine until you went all hydroponic and made it so strong."

"So now it's my fault? I thought you wanted more, more, more sales to save the convent," Sister Ethel says. "I didn't hear you complaining when we tripled production. Anyway, only Blythe says it's too strong."

"But what if she tells Margaret?"

"She can't very well tell Margaret at the moment, can she?"

"I suppose not. What a huge, unholy mess!"

"Pick, Rosie."

"What about Blythe's lunch?"

"I think she can eat a little later today, Rosie. Now pick and bag. I'll put on some music to keep us company."

My mind is tumbling, trying to understand what I just heard. The black skirts have stopped two tables away from us. My brain puts the pieces together like a caster gliding on the Ouija board, touching one letter after another until the truth becomes clear: S-I-S-T-E-R-S. Ms. Stillford hasn't been kidnapped by the rockers, or Owen Loney, or John Denby. She's been locked up by Ethelburga and Maria Giuseppe Rossello!

I put my hands to my head like I'm trying to keep my brain from exploding. Ms. Stillford's been here in the convent all along—locked up because of an argument over *the tea*.

The sisters begin rustling through the plant leaves while Sister Rosie mutters, "Oh dear, oh dear, oh dear."

I turn to tell Ella, but I'm so shook up that only non-words come out. "Muh muh muh muh muh."

She puts her hand over my mouth.

34

Bam! Bam! Bam!

Banging sounds from the front door. Thank goodness—Mom must be back.

The sisters rush out of the solarium and down the hall. Sister Ethel calls out to the visitor as she descends the steps: "Just a minute, just a minute. Coming."

Sister Rosie follows, saying, "Oh dear, oh dear, oh dear."

Bam! Bam! Bam!

Ella and I scramble out from under the plant tables. I'm torn between running down the hall, yanking open doors looking for Ms. Stillford, and following the sisters downstairs to meet Mom. Ella makes the decision for us and pulls me toward the staircase. We crouch down and peek through the spindles.

When Sister Ethel opens the front door, I hear Skullfinger say, "Yo, ladies. We're the buyers."

Speaking to the rocker in her doorway, Sister Ethel says, "Where's Margaret? We're not quite ready for a showing yet."

"She couldn't make it," Skullfinger says as he moves inside, crowding the sisters backwards.

"Do I smell smoke?" says Sister Rosie.

I lift my nose and sniff. There is a faint smell of smoke, and a siren wails in the distance.

"Oh, yeah," Skullfinger says. "There's a fire down the road. By those crappy old houses." Through a pair of spindles, I see that Stevie has entered the foyer. "She's probably down there, being the sheriff and all."

Uh oh. He knows Mom's the sheriff.

"A fire. Oh, my heavens," says Sister Ethel.

Cats are filing in through the open door as Skullfinger and Stevie take a few steps toward the stairway. Spiro runs up the stairs toward us.

"Okay, Sisters—if you really are nuns, that is," Skullfinger laughs. "No more real-estate shopping. You know what we want. So just hand it over—all of it. And while you're going through the trouble, we'll take your seeds, too."

A shiver slides down my spine as I realize the rockers aren't here for chalices or Virgin Marys. They're here for the tea.

Ella and I shrink backwards on our hands and

knees until we can try the first door atop the staircase, number one. Locked. We sprint to the second door on the right, number three. I hold my breath as I twist the knob. It opens. We dart in, and Spiro bounds after us. Ella carefully closes the door just as tattooed arms and flowing black fabric pass down the hall.

Inside the room, a desk is crowded with pictures of a family, all with round cheeks; a clock with a sunflower face; cookbooks; little figurines of Jesus with children or lambs; and bags of mini Halloween candy bars from, where else, Walmart. It has to be Sister Rosie's room. I rush to her window and see smoke billowing, ash flecking, police lights rotating, fire trucks spraying—chaos at the Abbott end of Mile Stretch Road.

In an instant, I'm dialing Mom's cell number. It rolls immediately to voice mail. I start to leave a message when I'm told, "This message box is full. Please try again later." Which never happens.

Sirens are still blaring outside. I realize that *this* is the rockers' way of keeping Mom busy.

"We have to keep looking in rooms," I whisper to Ella. "Ms. Stillford must be in one of them."

She nods agreement, and we open the door and sneak a look. The sisters and the rockers are in the solarium facing the plants. Their backs are to us.

We take a couple careful steps into the hallway. I'm about to whisper to Ella to try the door across from us when the rockers grab the sisters by their arms. It looks like they're turning to come back our way. We have no time to do anything except grasp the knob on door number five and pray it opens.

Ella's so close behind me that she steps on my heel as we slip inside.

"I don't think they saw us," Ella struggles to say.

I put my ear to the door. The sisters are pleading with the rockers—for what, I can't tell. When I turn to look around the room, I know immediately that it's Sister Ethel's. Two children dressed as a cowboy and cowgirl pose next to a pony in a yellowed photograph at a carnival. The cowgirl holds the reins. She has Sister Ethel's face. CDs of blues artists and stacks of books about running a business are piled on a table next to a computer.

I reach into my pocket for my phone, to call Dad this time. What? Not again! It's not there!

"Oh, no, no, no! I can't believe this!" I say. "I've lost my phone again!"

"You just had it a minute ago."

I look around and check all my pockets. "Forget it," I say.

Skullfinger's voice booms in the hallway. I crack the door open to hear better and peek.

"Open the door, *Sister,*" Skullfinger says to Sister Ethel. Stevie and Sister Rosie are behind them. Sister Ethel doesn't move. "Just open it, lady, and we'll get what we want and get out of here."

"I don't have the key," Sister Ethel says and tries to slip around him.

"Like I'm going to believe that." He grabs her wrist. "Stevie," he barks, "get the big one over here."

Stevie pushes Sister Rosie, and she lurches up to Skullfinger, almost losing her footing.

Skullfinger puts his face up to Sister Rosie's. "You two are testing my good nature. Now open that door."

Sister Rosie bursts into tears and hunts in her skirt pockets.

"What's in there, man?" Stevie tips his head to number ten.

"When we were in with the plants, they kept looking over here. Must be where they keep the seeds."

Sister Ethel says, "There's nothing for you in there. Everything you want is in the solarium. Take it all. I can't even understand why you want it so much, but take it and get out!"

Skullfinger grunts.

Sister Rosie finally fishes the key ring from her pocket, and Skullfinger grabs it. "Watch these two," he says to Stevie. He starts jamming one key after the other into the lock until he gets a match for door ten.

Sister Rosie whimpers.

Sister Ethel says, "No!"

Skullfinger twists the knob, flings open the door, and does a double take. "What the—? Stevie, look at this."

35

Skullfinger and Stevie hustle the sisters into number ten, and the door shuts behind them.

Ella and I inch into the hallway. Spiro paces near the solarium like an angry bear-cat, mewing his discontent. I strain to hear what's going on inside the room, but I can't make out Skullfinger's words. He's arguing with the sisters—and—OMG. It's Ms. Stillford.

My heart soars—she's safe. Wait! She's in there with the rockers—I have to save her!—and the sisters. I'm drawn in the direction of her voice, but Ella holds me back with a small, sympathetic, "I know, I know. Hang on."

A second later, Skullfinger and Stevie open the door.

I wave at Ella to turn back, and we run for Sister Ethel's room.

We hear the keys jangle in the hallway as Skullfinger locks door ten and says, "Bag as fast as you can. We'll deal with them as soon as we've got the all the stuff."

Deal with them! I scream in my head.

"What about Trinka and Bin?" Stevie whines. "They're supposed to bag the stuff."

"Bag the stuff. Now, man."

Okay. Think, Quinnie, think! What would Mom do?

Again, Ella opens the door and peeks in the direction of the solarium. "They're going in with the plants. I'll head down to where they locked up the sisters."

"Wait, let me look for—"

I scan Ethel's room. I think: *keys*, and my brain responds: *envelope.* I'm riffling through papers on Sister Ethel's desk when Skullfinger's booming voice startles me. I spin around and see—no Ella. She's gone.

"Yo, Stevie! The surprises just keep on comin'. Catch her."

I dive under the bed as the door to Sister Ethel's room bangs wide open. A split second later I hear Ella's voice from down the hall: "Get your hands off me!"

My ankle hurts like the devil from wrenching it on the leg of the bed. The rest of my body is petrified. As Skullfinger's boots pass within a foot of my nose, I resort to desperate hoping: *Don't look under the bed. Don't look under the bed. Don't look under the bed.* He pauses by Sister Ethel's desk and turns in a circle like he's looking around. I close my eyes. This could be it.

"I said get your hands off of me, you creep!" Ella's shouts are moving in the direction of the solarium.

"Ouch! Hey!" Stevie shouts. "I could use some help here, man."

"Can't you do one simple thing?" Skullfinger yells as he leaves the room.

I stay tucked under the bed.

"Gimme her," Skullfinger says.

"Put me down!" Ella yells.

"Stop kicking!" Skullfinger orders.

I picture Skullfinger's arm around her waist, carrying her down the hall like a log. In my mind, Ella's prying at his arm with her fingers. I hear, "Don't put me in that room. With. Those. Nuns!"

Thank you, Ella. She's telling what's going on.

I search my pockets one more time for my phone. If there was ever a time to call 911, this is it. But of course, my phone's not there.

New voices—female voices—float up the main staircase. I position my right eye to the door crack and watch pink-haired Trinka and blue-haired Bin walk by.

"We have to move fast," Trinka says. "That lobster guy spotted us walking up the beach from his boat."

"You let someone see you?" Skullfinger says.

"It's a big wide open beach," Trinka says. "You can't exactly hide on it."

"Shut up and go bag the plants."

"Yeah, yeah," Trinka says.

"Look, if we don't get this stuff to Martin, we can forget about going back to Moline."

The sounds of bickering gangsters and wailing emergency vehicles swirl in my head. Ms. Stillford *and* the sisters *and* Ella are hostages, and I can't call for help because I stupidly lost my stupid phone for a fourth stupid time. If I don't figure something out, I may never see them again.

Think, Quinnie, think!

Sneak out the front door and run for help. Sneak down the hall and somehow break into room ten.

My mind leaps back and forth. I run to the window and look out toward the fire. The cloud-licking flames are gone. The end of the road is a black billow, and the beach is blanketed gray with ash. My eyes move up the coastline toward—the *Blythe Spirit*? The boat is anchored about fifty feet from the convent beach. It rolls and bounces. Then I see Owen Loney, too—he's slipping over the gunwale into the icy water.

He's figured it out too. He must have followed Trinka and Bin up the beach.

But he doesn't know Skullfinger and Stevie are here.

36

I watch Owen Loney swim ashore, scramble up the rocks, and make his way to Our Lady of the Tides. That's all I can see from Sister Ethel's window before he disappears. But he'll be inside the convent soon. If I don't warn him, Skullfinger will catch him and deal with him too.

I assume Trinka, Bin, and Stevie are in the solarium bagging plants, but I don't know where Skullfinger is lurking.

I look around for something that will help me break into Ms. Stillford's room. A stool. No. A lamp. No. A basket. No. A picture. No. A bottle. No. An umbrella. Yes. That will have to do. A big black umbrella with a hard rubber handle.

I open Sister's Ethel's door with my left hand and squeeze the umbrella with my right. I can feel the metal ribs of the umbrella shift inside the folds of its slippery cloth. I poke my head into the hall and stop. There's music coming from the solarium. A recording of a woman's voice—singing "Trouble." It's the song the sisters and Ella sang in the driveway—when was that? A million years ago.

I start down the hall. All alone. To the locked room. To save my friends.

I flatten myself against the wall, but it doesn't matter. If any one of the gangsters looks down the hall, they'll see me. I just hope that shoving leaves—is it that maypop stuff?—into plastic bags to the tunes of Ella Marvell keeps them occupied. When I reach number ten, I hear muffled voices behind it. When I jiggle the handle, the voices go silent.

I drop to my knees and look in the keyhole. Something's blocking my view. I lean down and put my fingers under the door, but something blocks them too. It feels like a towel.

I put my lips to the crack between the door and the frame and whisper, "Ella?"

"Quinnie?" Ella says in a low voice.

"Is Ms. Stillford in there?" I whisper.

"Yes. Yes, she's here and she's fine."

"Quinn?" It's Ms. Stillford! Something flips in my belly when she says my name. "We've filled the key hole and blocked the space around the door so they can't get in. We're safe. Do you understand?"

"Yes."

"We're safe here. You just go for help. Get out of the convent and go for help."

"But Owen Loney is somewhere close. I should warn him!"

"Owen is here?"

"Yes. Somewhere."

"Get out, Quinnie. Owen can take care of himself."

She says that, but she hasn't seen Skullfinger.

I readjust my grip on the umbrella and crawl to the solarium doorway. Trinka, Bin, and Stevie are busy in the middle of the room, ripping vines from their pots and stripping their leaves. They've shredded their way through half of the gigantic sea of plants. I hear snatches of their conversation.

"He can be crazy-crazy," Trinka says.

"I think it's a bigger sin to kidnap nuns than regular people," Bin says.

"Shut up," growls Stevie.

"Remember that girl, Bin?" asks Trinka.

"What girl?" Bin says.

"The one from that café with the lobster fries. The one with the green eye shadow."

Stevie butts in: "Oh, we got her too. She's locked up with the nuns and that other one."

"What other one?"

"There's some other lady in there." He laughs. "I have *no* clue who she is."

"How many people you got locked up?" asks Trinka.

"A bunch."

"I wonder if that girl's got that eye shadow with her. I'd like to try it," Bin says.

"Right. You could become, like, friends," says Stevie. "And you could show her how to turn her hair green or something."

I almost drop the umbrella. These people are definitely not Einsteins. Ella Marvell starts to sing a new song. "You're my one, my one and only . . ."

"I like this one," says Trinka. "Turn it up. Turn it waaaay up. Go figure that those nuns would have some good jams."

I can't leave Owen Loney alone here with these creeps. That lobsterman thinks I'm a fool girl, and maybe I am, because I'm going to try and warn him, and my best chance is to get from the solarium to the back stairway and head him off in the kitchen.

So I start crawling through the table legs and tubes and wires. There's a new smell in the solarium.

It's more odorific than Ben's stinky old running shoes. Three sets of gangster feet are tapping their toes to Ella Marvell as I sneak past them. I check out Stevie's feet to see if they're the source of the disgusting aroma. Then I remember the leaves I smelled last night. When I'm almost there, my hip smacks into one of the tables and some of the plants rustle above me.

"Hey. What was that?" Trinka says over the music.

I don't move a muscle. Ella Marvell sings, "Till you walk out on me . . ."

"Probably a rat," Stevie answers and laughs. "Want me to go catch it for you? It'd make a good pet."

"Shut up, Stevie," Trinka and Bin say at the same time.

Stevie makes another wisecrack, and Trinka and Bin sing along with Ella Marvell to drown him out. I take the opportunity to scurry to the back stairway and scoot down the five steps to the landing.

The back staircase isn't big and beautiful like the one at the front. It's dimly lit, and the walls are close together all the way to the bottom.

Each board creaks even though I step carefully.

Each step brings more of the kitchen into view.

When I'm four steps from the bottom, I still can't see it all. A cupboard stands in front of me, piled high with newspapers and empty egg cartons. Someone upstairs turns up Ella Marvell to full volume. "And when you're gone, my one and only is me. Yeah, yeah. My one and only is me."

As I take the last step, the full kitchen comes into view, and I scream.

37

Skullfinger is waiting for me. Smiling. I'm paralyzed, except for the fact that my heart's snapping like a sail in a forty-knot wind.

"Well, if it ain't another one." Skullfinger looks at the umbrella in my hand. "You expecting rain?"

He beckons me to come all the way into the kitchen. I take small steps on wobbly legs. Skullfinger watches my every move.

My nose prickles from a briny smell. Next to the sink, there's a bowl of shucked clams, a bucket of clamshells, and a few potatoes. A half-shaved big Maine potato is turning brown on the cutting board. Next to it, there's a peeler and a few strips of potato skin. Chowder, mid-making.

As I inch farther into the kitchen, my brain races. I can rush to the sink and grab the potato peeler. Or, if he goes after the potato peeler, I can bonk him on the head with the handle of the umbrella. No. That won't work. He's a big guy. He probably flipped Ella off her feet like she was a broomstick.

Maybe I can talk my way out of this. They haven't harmed anyone yet. Just locked them in a bedroom.

Skullfinger nods like the wheels in his head are grinding too. "I suppose that boy's here?"

Where is Ben right now? School? The Abbotts? I hope he stays safely out of this mess.

"What's your name?" I ask. I try to sound calm and interested.

"What's *my* name?" He laughs. "What's *your* name?"

Okay, maybe a conversation won't work.

In the corner of my eye, I catch movement across the room. The handle of a green wooden door next to the fridge is turning slowly. It must be Owen Loney. It has to be Owen Loney. Please be Owen Loney.

I look away quickly and send mental messages to the lobsterman: go slow, stay quiet, sneak up behind Skullfinger.

"You can drop the umbrella," Skullfinger tells me.

No way. This umbrella is the only thing standing between me and his big tattooed arms. Skullfinger lunges at me, and I jump sideways. My eyes shoot to the green door, which isn't opening fast enough. Then, with one big adrenaline rush, I go all Mary Poppins and burst open the umbrella in Skullfinger's face. He tries to swat it down but I bop around, spinning it and thrusting it at him. Owen Loney finally throws open the green door with an "auyaahhhhhhhhh," leaps across the room, and jumps on top of the big man.

Skullfinger spins the lobsterman around and struggles to free himself, but Owen Loney hangs on with his feet off the floor. I close the umbrella and start smacking Skullfinger's legs with it. Toppled chairs skid around the kitchen. The big table's legs scrape the floorboards as it lurches in the struggle.

I hear the rush of footsteps, lots of them. I can't tell what direction they're coming from. I grab the bucket of clamshells and whirl around, looking for a clear shot at Skullfinger.

As I draw back for a throw, a cat runs in between my legs, and Ben bursts into the room. He scans the situation for a nanosecond then leaps into the fight. The clams pitch out of the bucket and onto the brawling bodies.

Amidst the grunts and the crunch of shells, more cats arrive. Dozens of them spill into the kitchen, jumping on the table and the counters. They investigate the stove, the clams, the clamshells. Spiro is snaking between my ankles.

Owen Loney wrestles Skullfinger to the ground and mounts his chest. Ben struggles to subdue the big man's thrashing legs. I slip-slide around them, frantically searching for anything I can use to hog-tie him.

Blood is pounding in my temples as I yank an extension cord out of a wall socket. I pull so hard that when the plug comes out, it sends me sliding backwards over clam juice, onto my butt. I have no time to be stunned. I roll to my knees and scramble over to the tangle of bodies, and while Ben and Owen Loney hold Skullfinger, I bind his hands. He twists and wriggles and tries to shake clamshells out of his hair. Owen Loney rips his belt out of his pant loops and cinches it around Skullfinger's ankles.

I turn to Ben and say, "Do you have your phone?"

He's already searching for it, but before he can press *9-1-1*, Mom, Officer Dobson, and two other police officers burst into the kitchen. Officer Dobson hustles over to Skullfinger and replaces the cord with handcuffs. "I got this bum," he says to Mom.

"Tell me quick, Quinn," Mom says.

"Upstairs. The other three are in the solarium, stripping the plants. The sisters, Ms. Stillford, and Ella are locked in the bedroom next to it—number ten." This information fires out of me like the facts in a sheriff's all-points bulletin.

Mom and the other two officers bound up the stairs.

Ben's breathless, and he has the makings of a bruise on his cheek. "Your dad had the Rook River Police trace your phone when we couldn't find you during the fire."

Oh, yeah. The fire. I remember the fire.

"This way," Officer Dobson says to Skullfinger and jostles him out of the kitchen.

Two more police officers rush in, and I point them up the stairs. I make a move to follow them when Owen Loney says, "Wait, Quinnie." It's part concern, part warning, and part order. "I'll go up first, to be sure they've captured the rest of them."

Everything in me wants to run past him. I want to be there when the door opens and Ms. Stillford is freed. I want to be the one to see her first. To grab her first. To hug her first.

"We'll hang here," Ben says and touches my arm like he thinks he might have to hold me back. Clam juice is running down his temple.

"I'll call down when it's safe," Owen says.

"I was worried about you guys," Ben tells me.

That kind of melts my heart. I admit, "Yeah, I was worried about us too."

"Come on up!" Owen Loney yells.

Ben and I kick our feet in gear and take the steps two at a time.

When we reach the second floor, the two officers who came in after Officer Dobson are leading Trinka, Bin, and Stevie out in handcuffs. Mom has smashed through the bedroom door, and everyone is hugging everyone. I push into the crowd and reach for Ms. Stillford.

I'm squeezing her around her waist, and she's got her arms wrapped around my shoulders. Somewhere deep down inside me, a knot relaxes, and as it comes undone, I'm sobbing and can't stop. And thank goodness nobody tries to stop me. Not Mom, not Ms. Stillford. Nobody is saying "it's okay" or "calm down" or "there, there." I just let it roll. When I finally look up, Mom's, Ben's, Ella's, and Ms. Stillford's faces are puffy and red. Even Owen Loney looks kind of choked up. And I love them all a zillion clamshells.

"I'm so sorry," I blubber to Ms. Stillford.

"Hush," she says and pats my hair. "What do you have to be sorry about?"

But there are so many things. I'm sorry I didn't figure out where she was sooner, I'm sorry that I thought Owen Loney was a psycho-killer lobsterman lover, I'm sorry I thought John Denby was dribbling wild rice soup down her chin, but all I can get out is, "I'm sorry I stole Owen Loney's gaff hook."

She looks at me and squints.

"Oh, I'm sure I'll get it back," says Owen Loney, who is now standing next to Ms. Stillford.

Ms. Stillford glances around the room, and her eyes narrow when she spots Sisters Rosie and Ethel. The nuns have inched apart from the group. "Not to worry, Quinnie," she says. "But I do know a couple people who have some serious explaining to do."

38

I can barely keep up with everything that happens next.

Officer Dobson and his deputies haul the Skullfinger gang off to jail in Rook River.

Mom wants to call an ambulance, and Ms. Stillford refuses. The sisters keep saying they are all right. Ella says she's fine too.

Mom tells the sisters and Ms. Stillford to come to her office tomorrow to give statements—after they've rested and had a chance to calm down. The sisters say they are calm, but they don't look it. Ms. Stillford takes a deep breath and says she'll be there. Some detectives who have arrived take pictures of the solarium, bag evidence, and stretch yellow crime scene tape around the convent.

Dad, John Denby, and Mr. Philpotts show up to collect us kids, while Ben notes that the yellow tape is made of "durable, resilient, tear-proof plastic."

* * *

The next morning, I ask Mom if the sisters are going to be charged with kidnapping Ms. Stillford. Mom doesn't tell me, but she does question the sisters in her office for a long time. I sneak down the stairs and press my ear to the closed door.

"Start from the beginning, Sisters."

"We are so sorry," Sister Rosie says. "We didn't mean any harm. We were frightened."

Mom presses them. "I understand that. I want to know how all this happened."

"Well." Sister Ethel's voice has more than a little worry in it. "All right, then, to go to the very beginning, the summer before last, the monsignor told us that the convent wasn't exactly making sense financially. I suppose that should have been obvious."

"And?" Mom says.

"And . . . ," Sister Rosie says, "he told us he might have to close it down and sell it, since the property has become so valuable. So, Sister Ethel and I decided we had better raise some money to save the convent. Ethel and I, we were talking to Blythe about the cats. Blythe wanted us to take them to the shelter—"

Sister Ethel cuts her off. "It's not about the cats, Rosie. We were telling Blythe we needed to raise

273

money, and she suggested we sell tea on the Internet. She's an expert gardener, you know, Margaret—and she created a tea for us to grow and sell."

"Speak up," Mom says. I realize she's recording their interview.

Sister Ethel continues, more loudly. "We didn't know how much more . . . potent the fertilizer would make it."

Sister Rosie adds, "And we'd been getting bigger and bigger orders from this one buyer. Very demanding about getting the tea on time. And when we got a little behind on his order, he threatened to come to the convent."

"And Blythe stopped by on Thursday at dinnertime," Sister Ethel continues. "She said she'd made a cup from the most recent batch, and she thought it was too strong."

"She wanted us to stop selling it and have it tested."

"Tested for what?" Mom asks.

"I don't know," says Sister Rosie. "To see if it's not safe to drive after you drink it, or something like that."

"We tried to explain that we needed to finish just this one order for this very nasty customer," says Sister Ethel, "but Blythe said if we didn't stop selling it she would tell you, Margaret, and we said we were shipping that day, and Blythe was standing in the solarium entryway, and we kept saying 'after this one order,' and she kept saying no—"

The room goes quiet, and I get ready to run for the kitchen. Then I hear a nose blowing like a Canadian Honker, and I realize that Sister Rosie is crying.

Sister Ethel says, "And we're not proud of this in any way, and we've apologized fifty ways from Jerusalem to Blythe, but we panicked and . . . *urged* her into the bedroom next to the solarium."

"Urged?" Mom asks.

"Do we need a lawyer?" Sister Ethel asks.

Mom's voice becomes a little more official. "You can have a lawyer at any time, sisters, but you are not under arrest. I am only trying to determine what happened."

"We'd like to think that Blythe was our guest," says Sister Rosie. "I fixed the room nicely and brought her lovely meals."

"When did she *become your guest*?" Mom asks.

"Oh, let me see," says Sister Ethel. "So much has happened. Yes. It was Thursday, about dinnertime, when Blythe uh . . . came to stay."

"Did you go to her house any time after that?"

Yes, Mom! Thank you for asking that.

"That was me," says Sister Ethel. "I went over Friday morning and cleaned and picked up a few things for her. She needed her medications."

"What about the letter that Blythe wrote to me? Do you know anything about that?"

It's so quiet for so long that I get nervous the door will fly open.

"Have you talked to Blythe yet?" Sister Ethel asks.

"I'm talking to her this afternoon."

"We'd really like to not comment anymore about Blythe at this time, if that would be okay with you, Margaret."

* * *

Mom and the sisters spend the rest of the morning in her office, mostly talking about the rockers and the Internet and the tea shipments. I lose interest when they reach the point where I know most of it. But that afternoon, when Ms. Stillford comes over to talk to Mom, I'm back at the door, all ears.

"Do you mind if I record this, Blythe?" Mom says.

"I do, Margaret. No recording, please."

"But—"

"I'll tell you everything in my own way, but no recording."

"Fine." Mom's tone is strained.

"The sisters needed some help raising funds," Ms. Stillford begins, "so I put together a little tea recipe for them. Mainly maypop, or passionflower. Actually it's *Passiflora incarnata*. I thought it was clever. They packaged it as Sanctity Tea. 'It's not only for relaxing, it's for giving.'"

Mom doesn't laugh, but I smile thinking about how tickled the sisters were when they told Ella and me about it.

"I showed them how to grow it hydroponically to get a fast yield, but they got some bat guano on their own. The next thing I knew, I brewed some, and *phew*, it was a very strong."

"So they enhanced the relaxation quality?" Mom asks.

"They didn't do it on purpose. But the minute I tasted it, while I was fixing dinner Thursday evening, I walked over there and told them not to sell it until we could find out if it was safe."

"What happened then?" Mom sounds eager.

Ms. Stillford is quiet. She's choosing her words carefully. "They . . . wanted to complete a big order and . . . I wanted them to hold off . . . and they *urged* me to stay with them and think about it."

"They *urged* you to stay?" I can hear in Mom's voice

that she can tell Ms. Stillford's using the same word as the sisters. "Have you talked to the sisters since—well—since you ended your little stay with them?"

"I have. I spoke with them last night."

I imagine the sisters and Ms. Stillford sitting in her living room, drinking tea—not Sanctity Tea—and talking over everything that happened. The sisters are so, so, so sorry, and Ms. Stillford is upset but understanding. That would be like her.

"What about the letter you sent me, Blythe?" That would have been my next question too, Mom.

"Hmmm." Ms. Stillford pauses as though she hasn't thought about the letter until this very moment. "I wrote the letter so no one would worry."

"If you were concerned about the rest of us worrying, why didn't you try to escape?"

"You kind of had to be there, Margaret. I thought it would be over as soon as they delivered their last order. It just . . . dragged on a bit."

"I don't know why you're doing this, Blythe," Mom says. "Covering up for them. Why? Kidnapping is a very serious matter."

"I'm not happy about this either, Margaret, but I refuse to press charges against these two women. What they did was foolish—stupid, even. But not malicious. I've suffered no real harm that I can't forgive in my own time, in my own way. Plus, they have a higher power to answer to."

Mom and Ms. Stillford have never argued about anything this serious before, but the conversation goes the same way as the others. They end up agreeing to disagree.

* * *

The next morning, Ella, Ben, and I are in Gusty's parking lot when we see the sisters riding out of town in the back of the monsignor's big black car. Sister Ethel is looking straight ahead with a stone face, like she's headed for the big day of reckoning, and Sister Rosie is staring out the window. When she spots us, she gives a feeble little wave. Later that day, the monsignor is in Mom's office for an hour, but I can't get within ten feet of it because Dad is home.

That afternoon, Mom, Mr. Philpotts, and John Denby take me, Ella, and Ben to the Rook River prosecutor's office, where we identify pictures of Skullfinger, Stevie, Trinka, and Bin. We might have to be witnesses at their trial, according to Ms. Durbin, the prosecutor. They're looking at charges for kidnapping, assault, terroristic threats, and on and on.

Ben immediately wants to know whether they

were selling the tea as a drug, too.

Ms. Durbin smiles. "Well, the combination of the hydroponic process and that fertilizer may have enhanced the natural sedative properties of the leaf, but these guys were not really interested in that. It turns out this maypop has such an unusual smell that, when used as a packing material, it fools the drug-enforcement dogs."

"They only wanted it for packing material?" I ask.

"Correct. But that only works until the dogs are trained on the scent, which they now have been, so their crime spree was all for nothing."

"What does it smell like?" Mr. Philpotts asks.

"If you mash it up, it smells like a really stinky old rubber shoe," Ms. Durbin says.

"I smelled that in the solarium," I say. "I thought it was Stevie's stinky feet." That gets a good laugh.

As we leave the office, we see the sisters walking in with the monsignor.

"I guess the sisters are witnesses too," I say to Mom.

"They sure are," Mom answers and shakes her head. "They are pretty darn lucky, if you ask me. They could very easily be here under different circumstances."

I know exactly what she means, and I know enough to let it drop.

39

I dread the time when I will have to face Mom and Dad about my part in all of this, but I know it's coming. It turns out the confrontation comes at dinner after we get home from the prosecutor's office. They've recovered from the fright of my being in the convent, and Mom is starting to figure out that I violated pretty much every order she gave me.

The meeting is so serious that Dad cooks dinner at home and Mom turns off her phone.

Dad slides a plate in front of me filled with buttered brown bread smothered in molasses baked beans. On any other night I'd dig in, but not tonight. Tonight my throat is closed up tight. I can't bring myself to spear even one bean with a fork tine.

Mom's beans are untouched too.

So are Dad's.

"I'll start," Mom says. She pushes her plate an inch

away from her. "This is not about me being the sheriff. I want to be clear about that first." She looks at me like she expects me to nod. So I nod. She continues. "It's about me—and your dad—being parents." They both look at me. I nod. She continues. "It's about the fact that every building in this town could burn down, and every valuable thing could be stolen, and every summer person could speed, and no one, I mean no one, could recycle—Gusty's could even go broke—and we wouldn't care, if it meant that you were safe."

I nod even though my head is down and tears are starting to fall from my eyes in big drops onto my shirt. I wait for Mom to say, "What were you thinking, Quinnie?" But she doesn't.

Instead she says, "I know what you were thinking, Quinnie. You were first and foremost concerned about Blythe's safety. I understand that. But can you see that Dad and I are first and foremost concerned about *your* safety?"

I look up just enough to see Dad gripping the handle of his knife so tightly that his palm has turned white. Something about this opens my sob dam. I keep expecting Mom and Dad to come over and hug me or put their arms around me, but they don't.

"I thought we'd lost you, Quinn." Dad's voice is throaty. "I was never so scared in my life."

It's quiet for a long time, and no one moves. Something tells me I should explain myself, defend myself, but something else tells me that's not what they want to hear. But I can't help myself.

"I'm not that kind of person, Mom."

"What do you mean?"

"I can't just sit by when I think people need me, when I think I can help."

"Which makes you exactly like your mother." Dad gets up and hugs me. "But you can't be sheriff yet, Quinnie. You're only thirteen."

Mom follows Dad up and wraps her arms around me. We're having a family hug-cry.

"I'm sorry," I say into Dad's shoulder.

"I'm sorry," Mom says into my hair.

"I won't do anything like this ever again," I add. "Not that way."

Mom backs up and holds me at arm's length. "What do you mean, 'not that way'?"

40

So, we work out a few things. I concede that I made some dangerous decisions that I shouldn't have. Mom concedes that she could have explained the investigation process to me better, so I didn't think that not enough was being done. Dad concedes that he will brew caffeinated coffee after noon since Mr. Philpotts has been complaining about it solidly for two weeks. But mostly, we all hope our mightiest that nothing bad ever happens in Maiden Rock ever again.

That's when Mom sets up a town coffee talk for the next day at Gusty's and invites everyone who helped in the search and rescue, and convent arrest, and Abbotts fire. It's kind of a Maiden Rock thank-you.

At eight thirty the next morning, Ella, Ben, and I walk down Mile Stretch Road toward the café. Cars cruise up and down like it's summer. Ella tells us how her dad gave her the "third degree," detective slang for interrogation, about this whole mess. "He was ninety percent yelling at me and ten percent gathering good stuff for a book."

By nine thirty, the Gusty's parking lot is almost full. Ella, Ben, and I settle in to our regular table.

"Hey," Ben says. "Guess how far underwater chocolate can be before a dog loses the scent?"

Ella and I look at each other and give him a coordinated eye roll. He laughs. "Well, if that's the way you're going to be, when you really need to know, don't ask me!"

Dad brings a plate of cinnamon buns to our table. "Anyone for a glass of good old milk?" he says.

"Oh, yeah. I could drink like a gallon," Ben says.

I can't wait for the action to begin. Mom told me there'd be a few exciting announcements.

Officer Dobson and some firemen come in. They shake hands all around and clap each other on the shoulders. A boy who looks like he's in high school holds the door open for a woman I don't recognize. She's ancient-looking, dressed all in black and leaning on a walker. Ben announces to our table, "That's Miss Prunella Abbott, last remaining direct descendant of the original Abbotts."

Ella says, "And *who* is that cute guy with her?"

"No idea," Ben says and shuts up.

The monsignor trails Miss Abbott, entering along with another woman, a younger woman in a white blouse, a sweater vest, and a short black headscarf.

"Who's she?" Ben asks us. Ella and I both shrug like we don't know.

"Everyone!" Mom yells above the chattering crowd. "Officer Dobson and I have a few things to report. Carl? You wanna come up?" Mom's least favorite police officer lumbers to the front of the room and stands next to her, holding his cap.

"First of all," Mom says, "I want to thank Officer Carl Dobson for helping apprehend the suspects."

The room erupts in applause, and Office Dobson actually blushes.

"Second, I'd like to report that the four perpetrators are being held without bail until a trial date can be set. You may have heard they were trying to steal the convent's supply of tea as an illegal-trafficking tool. For any of you who bought the tea, it's perfectly safe, but it doesn't have the most pleasing aroma.

"And now," Mom continues, "I'd like to turn the floor over to the monsignor, who has an announcement."

Heads turn to the monsignor as he stands up.

"Let me say, first, that the fright of the recent

events has focused the archdiocese's attention on the needs of the convent," he says. "So, I'd like to introduce Sister Cecilia." The young nun rises. "Sister Cecilia has an MBA, and she's going to come to Maiden Rock and manage the convent's renovations—and its transition to the new Maiden Rock Spiritual Center." He smiles and a few people applaud. "More importantly," he continues, "this is going to create a lot of construction jobs here in town, and we are very happy to announce a priority to local workers."

The crowd erupts with enthusiasm.

Mom steps forward again. "Okay, then. Thank you, Monsignor.

"Next. I'd like to give the floor to Miss Prunella Abbott, who has come here today, all the way from Auburn, to talk to you all about the fire. As you know, the Abbott family lost its entire compound here a few days ago, and we are all so very sorry for them."

Miss Abbott's young companion, who—I agree with Ella—is pretty cute, helps her stand and steady herself on her walker. Miss Abbott's voice is frail and hollow as she tells us about growing up in Maiden Rock and owing something to the town.

Mom comes to the rescue. "And Miss Abbott has a great surprise for us. The Abbott land will be dedicated to the City of Maiden Rock as an ocean-view park." She barely finishes the sentence when everyone starts clapping.

"And folks, before Blythe arrives, I'd like to ask for your cooperation and neighborliness in not asking her about her disappearance. She's been through an ordeal, and she's recovering at her own pace. More than anything, she needs our friendship, not our questions."

Everyone in the café nods. A silence hangs in the air until someone coughs, and the crowd falls back into buzzing about the new jobs and the park.

Dad's delivering an order of cinnamon buns to a table by the door when Ms. Stillford walks in . . . accompanied by Owen Loney. She has her arm through his arm, and the smile in her eyes says she's doing fine. Owen Loney pulls her chair out for her and goes for coffee. He walks up to the counter next to John Denby and puts his hand on John Denby's shoulder. And John Denby's lips get a friendly lop-sided twist!

Several people flock around Ms. Stillford, and pretty soon there is hugging and hand-shaking and folks slapping Owen Loney on the back. I hear "Congratulations!" and "That's wonderful" and "About time."

"What happened?" I ask to no one in particular.

A woman walking past our table says, "They're married."

My brain goes *zzt zzt zzt*. Ms. Stillford and Owen Loney are *married*? What about John Denby? I look at him and he's still smiling! *Zzt zzt*.

Mom is as shocked as everyone else. I hear her say, "But Blythe, why the secrecy?"

The crowd quiets while everyone listens for the answer.

Owen Loney says, "Out of respect for John. We were waiting for the right time to tell him."

"Which was not necessary," John Denby says and waves his hand. "But I appreciate the thought."

More people walk over to congratulate the happy couple.

All this time, Ella's dad is sitting at the counter scribbling in a notebook. I assume he's jotting ideas for his next novel. Maybe Monroe Spalding will learn a thing or two from the *Mainahs* in Maiden Rock.

I find my way to Ms. Stillford, and she puts her arm around my shoulder.

"Big news, yes?" she says.

"I don't know how much more big news this town can handle."

She leans back and looks at me like she's trying to

decide if I'm happy for her or not. "Name the feelings, Quinnie."

"When did you get married?"

"We got married about three months ago in Rook River."

I lean my head on her shoulder. I am happy for her, but I want to know that things won't change with us. I want to ask that, but I can't find the exact way to do it. I say something I really believe.

"I think he's a nice man." I don't mention anything about the lady I overheard calling him an old coot because I think that might hurt her. Or maybe she would laugh—I'm not sure.

She squeezes my shoulder.

"He thinks the world of you, too."

"He does?" I'm shocked. "Even after the gaff hook? And the boat? And his shirt?"

"What about his shirt?"

"Uh, never mind. I'll explain it all later."

"I'm not going to be any different as a teacher, Quinn. School won't change."

That's when I notice that she's wearing the ring that I saw on her dresser, the one I thought was from John Denby twenty years ago. I realize that if she's been married to Owen Loney for three months, then all summer she's been the same Ms. Stillford to me.

But I have to tell her about a flaw in her statement.

"There will be *one* change."

She turns to face me. "Can you give me a hint?"

"Just wait until you get to know Mariella Philpotts."

She laughs—a little nervously. "Oh?"

"She's not Zoe, but she's . . . cool. Very different but cool." I grin, and she ruffles my hair.

Now that I know Owen Loney no longer thinks I'm a fool girl, I really want to ask him about the blood on the shirt and his taking the laundry out to sea. Still, I figure that can wait for later, since this has turned into a wedding celebration. But he walks up to me and says, "Quinnie, you handled yourself pretty well in that kitchen."

"I'm sorry about taking your gaff hook off the boat and thinking you were a maniac psycho-killer lover."

He nods and reaches in his pocket and hands my phone to me—again.

I'm stunned. "Where . . . ?"

"In the convent's upstairs hallway. I saw it when we all left."

"Thanks." I look at it and see fifteen missed calls and ten text messages. I scroll the text messages— Ben, Ben, Ben, Ben . . . Anonymous.

Sometimes you've got to trust before you know the truth.

I glance at Ella, and a moment later, she is at my side. "I've got something for you."

She sticks her hand out to offer me a small nail-polish bottle filled with a deep-purple lacquer. "*Goth Goblet Grape.*"

She's smiling. She should do that more often. It shows off the blue of her eyes better than eye makeup. "Tell the truth. You sent the texts, didn't you?"

She nods her head. "Guilty."

"What about the one when we were in your room?"

"So, there's this way to write texts and then tell the app when to send them."

"But why anonymous? Why didn't you just tell me?"

"Uh, hello, I tried. But you were convinced that neither Monroe Spalding nor I had anything valuable to add to your investigation."

I think back on all the times I rolled my eyes. "Fair enough."

It isn't long before everyone in the café is busy talking about Ms. Stillford and Owen Loney's upcoming wedding reception and the new Spiritual Center. Ben says he has something to tell me and pulls me over to the corner.

He leans in close and drops his voice in a secret-telling kind of way. I feel a little dizzy.

"That blood on Owen Loney's T-shirt? A shark jumped in his boat, and he had to club it to death. He took the clothes into Rook River, to a laundromat, because he didn't want to get caught washing his clothes in Ms. Stillford's house."

Here I thought Ben was going to kiss me, but instead he's giving me detailed information about the case. But for some inexplicable reason, I'm not disappointed. Actually, up close like that, I notice a couple lone hairs growing on his upper lip. Almost like a catfish. And he smells of soap. And he doesn't smell of soap in an I-want-to-kiss-him kind of way. Maybe, for now, I'm happy to be more like a cousin.

"I just thought you'd want to know," he says.

"You're right. I did want to know," I say.

Ben doesn't step away, but he tilts his head to watch Ella. She's talking to the cute guy who came with Miss Abbott. He hesitates a second, then walks across the café and joins their conversation. And snap, I miss Zoe. But I also admit I'm looking forward to being snowbound this winter with the blue-eyed, blues-loving girl from New York City. At the very least, Maiden Rock will be cosmetically colorful.

Acknowledgments

Thanks to my family, and especially to Chuck
Hanebuth and Magda Surrisi for generous reading and
commenting on early drafts. To VCFA, the entire faculty
and administration, and especially to my advisors Matt
de la Pena, Tim Wynne-Jones, Rita Williams-Garcia,
and Tom Birdseye. To my writer buddies, especially
The Magic Ifs, my magic critique group; Sue Cowing,
Patricia Godfrey, Lin Oliver, Lynne Wikoff, Tammy
Yee; and my VCFA and SCBWI tribes. To my reader
buddies, especially Kaye Walsh, Beth Worrall Daily,
and Amy Spooner-Apa.

Gratitude to Greg Hunter, who enriched this book with editorial wit and wisdom and helped it find an audience. To my agent, Linda Pratt, who is my friend as well as my champion. To Ingrid Sundberg, who created a map that matches my imagination. To Gilbert Ford, who put the perfect face on Maiden Rock.

About the Author

C. M. Surrisi lives in Asheville, North Carolina, with her husband Chuck, two rascal Cavalier King Charles Spaniels named Sunny and Milo, and Harry, the Prince of Cats. She is a graduate of the Vermont College of Fine Arts MFA program in Writing for Children and Young Adults. *The Maypop Kidnapping* is her first novel. It draws from her memories of summers in Maine.